I0677834

Cultivating the Texas Twister Hybrid

a novel

by

Michael Lyons

HiT MoteL Press

www.hitmotel.com

Library of Congress Cataloging in publication Data

Lyons, Michael
        Cultivating the Texas Twister Hybrid
I. Title

ISBN: 0-9655842-0-8

Published by HiT MoteL Press

Designed by Michael Lyons

In memory of my sister Joanne

"The greatest service which can be rendered any country is to add a useful plant to its culture." —Thomas Jefferson

Cultivating the Texas Twister Hybrid

The Land

1

CATMAN LANDS ON HIS FEET IN A DOGWALK HOUSE

I had a farm once. It was just a little farm I rented for a season near Manor Texas, outside of Austin. I got it in a kind of partnership deal with Greg, Lenora's son, because the farm was in his name and he was the master grower and he turned me on to the farm under condition that we grow marijuana on it and split the crop.

I moved out to the farm on a cold clear day, February the second, 1977. As I didn't have a car, I got a friend to truck me and the stove out there. The farm house was up a rutted, quarter-mile, dirt road driveway. It was bleak in that clear winter light. The winter wind was a constant low level swirling howl. The few trees around the little house were denuded. I was too broke to have the electricity turned on although there was a pole out to the house.

I did have enough money to buy a used wood-burning stove made of tin and a new long handled axe with a double-edged blade. There were many big wood piles on the place with enough cedar logs to split and burn to last through several winters. I would live by candle and fire light. It would be like living in the dark ages where all a man had to do was chop wood and haul water. I was making the best of the poverty situation by going into a Zen phase and simplifying my life. I was going to get back to the basics.

I had the window rolled down and heard the crunch of car tire on gravel as me and my old friend, a man I had grown up with since junior high, slowed to a stop in front of the porch at the end the meandering driveway.

It was a brave little house, looked like a paddle wheel ship plying its way through a rolling sea of tall grass. The gingerbread trim along the roof line decorated the porch with a delicate fancy touch from the old country. It made the house look strangely out of place, as if it had been picked up by a tornado from somewhere else and plunked down in the middle of the prairie. The paint job, once white to reflect the heat, was now yellowed and peeling in places. I had to take a double step onto the porch—the top step was missing.

I opened the screen door against the solid ca-thunk of its c-clamp. Rattling the big skeleton key in the old-time keyhole, I unlocked the front door and entered the hallway. My friend didn't even come inside. He leaned against the car fender, smoking a cigarette looking at the bleak winter landscape.

My bootsteps sounded hollow down the dark brown hall of faded wood. The house moved and creaked as I walked into it. Outside the wind stayed at bay, banished by the house. Yet the wind's muffled howling could still be heard outside, probing the house through walls and windows

I poked my head into the first room off the hall. There was a bed in there. It had a window looking out to the front of the house and another looking out to the side. I walked past its door a step or two down the hall. I passed another door on the right side of the hall. It opened into a large square room. I continued down the hall to the kitchen, which was a big bright yellow room at the back of the house. Some country woman, probably Greg's girlfriend, had loved that room. The kitchen had a sink, but no running water. As I walked back through the house, I noticed there was no inside bathroom. I went back into the big square room. Someone had taken its walls down to the bare boards. The big square room stuck out of the long part of the house and had windows in the three outside walls, some of which were missing glass. The house had been rained on and rained in.

Birds fly in and birds fly out, I thought.

In the kitchen I heard a rodent or some small animal bolt across a counter, making a little scratching sound.

I slowly moved my eyes across the cupboards and the shelves of the old stove. A pair of rodent eyes met mine. Whisker faces! There!

"Skatt!" I shouted, flipping my hand at the critter.

There was a scuttling of rats in the house. Little furry animals darted into a crack. Yes, there were rats. They had set up nests in the shelves of the old propane stove. Outside had started to move inside. I was worried about snakes and scorpions. I wondered what kind of creatures were looking back at me out of these old uninsulated walls.

Back outside, my friend helped me unload the stove and some shiny black lengths of new stovepipe. As we settled the ducting on the ground in front of the porch, the wind, swirling all around, made deep organ noises blowing across the openings.

"Walker, I've got to be gettin' back to town," he said.

I hated to see him go. My old friend gave me a quizzical look as he turned to get into his car. "You gonna be all right out here?" he said.

"I'll be fine," I said, putting on a brave smile. Even my old friend thought I was slipping into darkness. However, I had a lot to do before sundown. I had to get some wood chopped and a fire started before night, otherwise I would have to do it by flashlight.

The first room, with the bed, would be mine. It had glass in the windows and a working flue. I got the stove and pipe assembled, and brought in several armloads of wood before it was dark. I stacked enough wood to last the night in the corner beside the stove.

This was my first realization: I would get doubly warmed: once by chopping the wood and again by burning it. After laying a fire in the stove, I dragged a kitchen match hard across the stove top. With a splitting rip, the tiny flare ignited the twilight gloom. A crackling fire soon took the chill off the place.

I lay down in the old bed. It was so soft that it rose up on either side around me. It was like lying in a trough and trying to look over the waves of the ocean. I would have to struggle amid spring sprongs to climb out of it.

So. This was to be home for a while. It wasn't much, but at least I wasn't homeless. I heard the rats in the kitchen but I would take care of them tomorrow. I thought about the recent past that had brought me to this.

A love affair in Montreal had gone bad. I had just hitchhiked across America back to Austin in the dead of winter to escape it.

I had been hopping from one friend's house to the next, crashing a night here and a night there and it was getting old. I had been living this kind of life for what seemed like forever: taking off on transcontinental hitchhiking trips only to be pulled back to the laid-back lifestyle of Austin.

At the time I lived a nomadic life. Which is a euphemistic way of saying I, Walker Underwood, was once a homeless person. I know now I had low self-esteem and restlessness and made a virtue of not asking much out of life. I called it a nomadic life. Call it what you like. Living the way I did, shifting around a lot, not taking care of things until you absolutely had to, really kept you on your toes. I thought of myself as Catman, the embodiment of the hippie ideal, capable of picking up and hitchhiking across the country at a moment's notice, moving in and out of scenes, able to land on his feet no matter what. I had been living like this ever since dropping out of high school. I had moved to Canada to become a ski bum and avoid the draft, then began enrolling in colleges. After attending several, and changing my major many times, I managed to get a degree in physics. But I had always wanted to be a writer.

When I was in Austin, I spent part of every day in the closed stacks of the UT Austin library. The infamous tower of the Cambridge of the Plains was my second home. Sometimes I worked as a teaching assistant—T.A.—the world's second oldest profession. I tutored jocks and wrote student papers for money. It is easy to do that in Austin.

The immediate precipitating incident that made me homeless was an insulting question from a roommate.

"What do you do with yourself all day?" he asked in a kind of sneering tone.

I had been renting a part of the porch of this old mansion from him. The roommate leased the whole top floor of a huge southern Victorian mansion on the corner of 6th Street and Enfield in Clarkesville, a part of Austin. In fact, it was through him that I met Ruth. Ruth lived next door. She was a seamstress and I paid her to do a little sewing for me. Ruth was a good old girl in her late 30s, a little on the heavy side. She liked to drink that Shiner Boch beer. She was Jewish, had been raised in Virginia. She had a marvelous head of curly hair. She had obviously spent some time in New York, because she had that "I don't take any shit off anybody" New York attitude.

"What *do* you do with yourself all day," the roomate had said in that kind of superior way the workers of the world have.

It really pissed me off. You have a lot of that in Texas, there's a kind of paterfamilias attitude. You hear the phrase, "We'll give him something to do," or "Have you got enough to keep yourself busy?" It made me want to ask, don't you people have any intellectual, artistic or spiritual interests to pursue. I was, however, plagued with ambivalence and lacking in ambition. One thing is for sure: I was definitely bummed out over the ending of this affair in Montreal.

"That does it," I said to the roommate. "I'm out of here."

I packed up my few belongings and put my tall skinny six-foot-three self out onto the street. In those days I could get everything I owned—a few pairs of jeans, some underwear and the rest, books and manuscripts—into a small backpack. It always felt good to pack up and move.

In my late 20s, and a struggling writer trying to learn my craft, I was obsessed by a novel I was working on called *Sex is the Anti-Gravity of Metamorphosis*. It was about my relationship with the woman in Montreal. I was writing this novel because I really did love the woman and what had happened to me in this relationship, and I wanted to enshrine her in art for all time. Moreover, I wanted to learn something about relationships from rehashing the incidents—I had been morbidly reliving every fight and passionate make-up for months since the breakup over and over in my mind—while they were still horrendously fresh. Also the story had lots of good sex, drugs, and rock and roll.

I was not your typical jobless college graduate. I was not just still hanging around the college town because there wasn't enough opportunity to get out. I was a philosopher monk living alone on the land, finishing my romance novel. She really had been a big influence on my life. I believed she had caused me to flower, had caused me to undergo metamorphosis from a frog into a prince, or so I hoped the book would prove.

For the winter it was just me out there, all alone. Once Ruth came out and spent the night but it was not the kind of place most women like. After it warmed up a bit and the growing season started, both Ruth and Greg came out more often.

At first the nights all alone in the little house way out on the prairie were terrifying. It was one thing to be there in the day, but at night walking through that lonely old house with just a candle or a flashlight splaying off the corners, throwing shadows, was pretty spooky. At night I heard the swirling eddies of wind currents howling all around the house and slipping in though the gaps in the structure where the walls met the floors. Even though it had been lived in by Greg for years and Greg had even lived there for a while with his girlfriend, I thought I could sense the ghosts of the old people who had lived there for years before them — little old black people who left their wearing on the walls just by their movement through. She so bent over double that she walked with a big walking stick, (thump step, thump step) through the swaying creaky house. She shuffled, shawl shrouded, surrounded always by her many cats purring in and out around her legs and running ahead of her. I found myself wondering about the relationship between this old couple. Somehow I knew Her took care of Him. But really, it was just the wind rattling the corrugated tin sheets wrapped around the bottom of the house. The house is raised up a couple of feet off the ground on stubby cedar posts, so the breeze can slip under the it. In the winter you covered up this gap between the house and the ground with long sheets of corrugated tin.

It was a dogwalk house. The hallway was really a breezeway through the middle of the house. If you opened both doors at each end of the hall, the wind would blast through. A dog could walk through the house without actually being inside the house. This is a good design for keeping cool. It lets the wind touch 3 and sometimes all 4 sides of a room. Perfect for the long hot summers, but less than ideal in February. The inside of that barren house was cold without mercy in February, when those northers came through. A thick heavy cold that hung in the air. The wind almost never rested. There was always its swish and play in the trees, its push and twirl in the reeds.

2

RUTH

Ruth came out once during February and we slept together for the first time. She just showed up at the land one cold afternoon and parked her yellow Dodge with the vinyl black top against the clear blue sky. She brought a 6-pack of cold Shiners, and after drinking beer and smoking pot we both decided it was too far for her to drive home and fell into bed together. Damn I was glad to have her warm body in my bed.

Until that time we had just been friends. It was a good relationship for both of us: Ruth was chubby and self conscious about her weight and I was trying to get past the playboy model syndrome and liked her cherubic zaftig look. At the time she was a cook at the Revolutionary Woman's Co-operative Munch House in Austin. Ruth would occasionally have me meet her at the back door of the kitchen when business was slack. Ruth would appear in double breasted white chef's coat and let me in. We'd set up a picnic under the trees and eat a meal in the afternoons, talking.

She had a lovely voice and spoke calmly with a lingering sibilant S that seemed to hang in the air for several seconds after she spoke. We mostly talked about spiritual stuff. Ruth was a very spiritual person and we would always get into these philosophical spiritual conversations.

We were neighbors in the Clarkesville of old, the Clarksville before the roads were paved. The house she rented was down toward the end of 6th St. near the river, not far from the Married Student Housing and the Old Confederate's Home. There weren't any more old confederates up there, but it was a stately mansion overlooking what must have been a vast plantation. Clarkesville had once been slave quarters, and there were all these funky little wood frame houses, connected by well-worn paths, and a few dirt roads. Blacks mostly and hippies and white trash and a few landed white gentry, lived in this part of Austin. She lived on a dirt road next to a house full of bikers.

Ruth was a classical Austin slacker. Basically a woman with her own creative life, she could take it or leave it where sex was concerned, and who had a great interest in drugs, art, getting high, dancing—not necessarily in that order. She had a beagle named Bugle.

I didn't really get to know Ruth all that well. I was too concerned with my own self. (I was kind of a sad case in those days, still actively hung up on the chick in Montreal, planning my triumphant return.) It was a pretty hard time all around. I was determined to build a place for myself in the country. I was looking forward to moving into what I thought was a marijuana economy. I was going to go outside the man made legal system and become engaged with the system of Nature's law. Not that I went around advertising this shift in persuasion; it had come about from a gradual erosion of my sense of who's in charge, over a long period of time, starting with not being able to trust teachers, priests, police, and doctors and moving on from there to being suspect of most everything.

Now Ruth had one especially good friend: Rose. The two were inseparable. Rose was from poor white background and had rawboned good looks with flaming red hair. She was a real hellion.

For a while there I was Ruth's boyfriend and I could tell Rose was all for it. It wasn't that Rose liked me for myself — I appeared to be such a serious fellow to her — but she was happy that her best girlfriend had a boyfriend. Now we could do stuff in couples. Like Ruth, Rose had a spiritual side. I first met Rose and her boyfriend in a teepee.

Ruth and Rose were great friends and they got up to all kinds of energy and wildness whenever they two got together. These sisters were so *bored* with their waitress and cook jobs, that they used to go into the walk-in and inhale the nitrous oxide that came in the cans of Redi-Whip. On the Redeye-whip they teased and provoked and hit on and horsed around with each other. Some times they got into hysterical falling down laughing jags which were singularly unlady-like to witness — they were like two fleas in a fit. Rose would engage in mounting behavior, by enclosing one of Ruth's legs between her own thighs and comence to hump on her. Ruth would act out in mock umbrage, at this and yell, "Fuckin' get offa me, bitch." Then the two women would swoon and collapse into each other amidst gales of guffaws and horsey laughter.

They would be pinching and pushing and shoving each other, walking arm and arm being loud and putting their business into the street, going "O, Yeah! and "Yeah!" back and forth arguing about something. Ruth ran with some wild women in a feminist Earth Mother peyote cult. They made long ritualistic trips down to the Mexican boarder around McAllen, and out west to Odessa to visit secret sacred places where they picked peyote. Ruth was one of the only people who could almost always be counted on to lay her hands on peyote. She even grew it in little clay pots. She gave me a couple of big cushiony plants, and said, "If you take care of these, they will take care of you."

This part of West 6th Street in Clarkesville was pretty much uncivilized at this time. Ruth had all kinds of friends out there. Every one was a mechanic working on a vehicle in the front yard, in the vacant lots around their houses, and in parking lots. They were all welders, she was one herself. The one thing they all seemed to have in common was they were dog people. Seemed like everyone in Austin had a dog.

Ruth shocked me one day. "Come with me," she said. I ducked under some overhanging branches and followed her between two houses into a neighbor's house for something, maybe some weed. The living room of the house had every surface, horizontal and vertical covered with leather. There were big swatches of black cowhide leather covering the walls. The tablecloths were squares of chamois draped over the dark wood. The chairs were all upholstered in leather. Even the lamp shades were made of some kind of skin. The house belonged to a gang of gay bikers who were deep into leather. Apparently she was a favorite. It gave me the creeps to see a whole room done up in leather. You didn't see too much of that kind of thing in Austin.

It was after an incident with Bugle and the dog pound that I really started to like Ruth. She had two dogs that she would bring out to the land with her. One was an amazing beagle dog named Bugle. She loved that dog. Very smart dog. Had been to college. That's where she got him. From the University of Texas animal lab where he had been undergoing various kinds of torture. He had been named Bugle because of the way he lead the charge in front of the pack, doing a steady roo-oo-rooo kind of bark, going crazy sniffing the winds and chasing animal trails.

Bugle could actually smile at you, genuinely pull back his lips in a smile. One moment you would not be looking at him and the next moment you looked over at him, and there he was—smiling at you. Bugle did it by pulling back his black gums on one side, showing a little teeth. There was something, some inflection perhaps, in the angle, of the way he curled the lip up, that made it, just pushed it over into a smile.

Sometimes Bugle's smile was a whimsical delight. Other times it appeared to be a horrible kind of Death's-head smile, a terrible kind of "little dog looking up at the shadow of humanity falling across the landscape and seeing its folly" kind of smile. It was the way a small old man would smile if he had become a dog. Or the way a dog would smile if it had become human. There was something goading and yet sympathetic in the smile. Whenever you saw it you couldn't help but think of where Bugle had come from and that he learned how to smile like that to charm his captors at the animal lab.

The city dogcatcher caught the Bugle again one day.

"Jesus Christ! You know what happened?" Ruth said.

"No, no, I don't."

"Oh, god damn it!"

"Whatssa matter?"

"They picked up Bugle. He's down at the pound! I looked all over for that dog yesterday."

"Oh, yeah?"

"Yeah. I called them on the phone, to find out if they had picked up a beagle. When I went down there to check for him they had him. They said, 'We can't release your dog until you pay the bill for the shots and the fine.' They told me I've also got to have an approved leash."

"Damn. Well how much is the fine?"

"They want 19 bucks a shot for two shots," she said, "distemper and heart disease, and the fine is twenty dollars. 'And we have a leash here you can buy for twelve dollars,' they said."

"Wow."

"There was Bugle throwing himself at the cage wanting to get out of there. That's almost sixty dollars. I don't have that kind of money.

"I was about ready to really get into this woman's face, but then I decided, ah fuck it, I'm just gonna calmly go away and get Rose and we're gonna come back and bust the Bugle out of there. I cased the place out. The cage doors didn't have pad locks. They just have these latches with little pins in them. There is a big gap between the top of the wall and the roof of the breezeway, which runs along the rows of cages. That wall gives out onto the lawn beside a parking lot in front of the pound.

"I'm gonna go in there and open the cage and snatch him and push him over the wall to Rose, and then run like hell out of there."

Ruth looked at me straight.

"You wanna come along and drive the getaway car?"

"I guess so, sounds like a plan."

"Let's pick up Rose," she said.

"OK." I said. "Let me daub a bunch of mud from the garden over the license plate in case they give chase."

"Good idea."

"Although a black and yellow Dodge might not be that hard to find," I said.

The plan worked. It was the funniest thing in the world to see the beagle flying through the air off the top of that wall, his long ears flapping in the breeze, as he fell into Rose's outstretched arms.

Rose caught him. She held him close to her as she ran to the car.

I had the motor running. I opened the door for her and pushed the seat out of the way and Rose and the Bugle clamored into the back seat.

We heard a loud, "Hey, you! You can't do that!" from inside the wall and then saw big Ruth squeezing herself through the gap between the top of that wall and the roof of the breezeway. She had climbed up on a table and boosted herself out the same way as the Bugle. I had the motor running. She dropped down to the lawn and come running puffing red-faced toward the car, as Rose and I waited a slow motion eternity for her. As soon as she was inside, I gunned it on out of there.

14

3

GREGORY AND THE F-1 TEXAS TWISTER HYBRID

Greg came out to the land near the end of the second month. He stepped out of his dark blue Camero carrying a small briefcase and wearing CIA-issue aviator's sunglasses. Standing there dressed like a typical Austin dude, jeans, cowboy shirt with swirls and snap-pearl button-down pockets—though *never* cowboy boots—tall and slender with a briefcase, he looked like some kind of cross between a cosmic cowboy and a spy. I was an old friend of Greg's mother and had seen Greg around over the years but we had never engaged each other in any conversation to speak of. I had the impression Greg was sullen, and Greg probably thought I was another one of his mother's flaky hippie friends.

Even so, I felt somewhat fatherly toward Gregory. The boy had long fine elegant red-brown hair that draped down to the middle of his back. He looked like a cowboy hippie version of Durer's Angel of Melancholy, his blustery continence and sneering harassed look hid a red tempestuous humor swirling beneath its surface. Like Ruth, Gregory was a study in contrasts too. Even though Gregory tried always to look laid-back he was one of the hardest working people I had ever met. He spent much of every day working in wood doing fine carpentry, even restoring antiques. Gregory owned his own house and filled it with carpentry tools. Yet even though he was a homeowner and solid citizen, Gregory was a consummate pot head, smoking probably a dozen joints a day. This had no effect on his attitude, he was very conservative. He looked down on sentiment, was imperious. He was a methodical person and did what he did very well. What he did best of all was grow pot. Because he smoked pot all the time, and probably had as high a tolerance for marijuana as anyone who ever lived, he needed to grow the best marijuana to ever come out of Texas.

Greg wanted to make sure the patch got started right. He was going to show me how to germinate the seeds.

In the funky yellow kitchen, Gregory snapped the clasp opening the briefcase. Inside, it was partitioned off into little cubicles each containing a little glass container about the size of a film canister with a black screw on top. Each little canister was filled with seeds and had a label affixed to it with the date of acquisition, type of marijuana, and the genetic source if it was a hybrid. He had developed these seeds from years of growing pot.

In particular some of the seeds were labeled with a big F-1.

"What's this F-1?" I asked.

"It means that the plants we are going to grow from these seeds are supposed to have what they call hybrid vigor."

Greg was very proud of his knowledge but always divulged it sparingly, speaking slowly and enunciating each word clearly and distinctly in his Texas twang, drawling out the main words for emphasis as if he were talking to an idiot, barely able to hide a sneer of contempt for those ridiculous enough not to have figured this stuff out for themselves the way he did. Greg always made me feel inferior around him even though I had been to college and he had not. Gregory began to explain: "You got two kinds of breeding. Inbreeding and outbreeding.

"If you use the males to pollinate the females from the same plant—like suppose I got some Hawaiian that I really liked, and it has some seeds, and if I grew those seeds into plants and let them pollinate each other and grow seeds—then that would be *inbreeding*.

"But if you plant the seeds from two *different* kinds of pot—say a Thai, and a Colombian and you cross pollinate them—you get a *hybrid*, and that's *outbreeding*. It turns out that hybrid seeds, what they call the first generation or F-1 generation, from *that* cross pollination, have hybrid vigor. They are bigger and stronger and stonier than the parents."

"That's what I'm after, hybrid vigor," he said with the slightest smile of satisfaction.

"But at the same time we want to grow sinsimilla, all females, because they are a lot stonier. We want them to put all their energy into making THC, not in making seeds. But you got to keep the parent seed stock up. So you do that either by inbreeding, or keeping a steady supply of seeds from all over the world, or you can make cuttings and clone them. I do that too."

"Cloning! You do cloning?" I asked, impressed.

"Yeah, I'll bring some out here."

We started the seeds germinating there in the kitchen by carefully placing bunches of each kind of seed into a folded, wet, paper towel. These folded towels, which were laid out flat onto dishes, had to be kept moist but not so wet as to drown the seeds.

As we did this, Gregory continued my orientation: "We've got seeds from all over the world sprouting here and you've got to keep track of them all the way through the process."

Gregory began attaching labels with the names of the seeds to the dishes. "Colombian, ganja, Thai, Panama. I plant only the best," he said with a prideful smirk.

Here is my kind of dope fiend, I thought.

I turned toward Gregory, made a dramatic audible sigh, gave him a big conspiratory smile and began to recite—as if it were a kind of beatnick poem spoken in a kind of singsongy British accent that people from India have—"Ganja... sativa... marijuana... blunt... spleeff... rainy day woman.... Sometimes there is merit in reciting the names of God."

This cracked him up.

When we were done and had them all labeled, Gregory said, "Now we'll be able to see how these sprouts do and plant only the most vigorous ones,"

4

A MAN OUT STANDING IN HIS FIELD

During my time alone on the land I kept himself busy with the basics of survival. This was a good thing too because it kept me from being inside my head.

Generally I took care of the place. The house hadn't been lived in for a year and there was much to do. The Bureau of Rodent Control in Austin, had a fiendishly diabolical, savagely direct and extremely efficient way of doing in the rats. They gave away packets of corn meal laced with powdered glass. It is a little known fact that rats can't regurgitate. When the rats ate the mixture, they suffered internal lacerations, and left the house to search for water. They never made it back.

The house had four rooms including the kitchen. It was shaped like an L. The open part of the L was a back yard, in the center of which was a large tree, shading over all that yard. Gregory had laid out concentric rings of bricks, setting each one level by hand making a circular patio radiating out in all directions from around the tree. There was a big picnic table under the tree and chairs. It was an inviting place.

I started my garden beside the house by hauling many 5 gallon pickle bucket loads of dirt from out back where the barn had burnt down. This dirt was a mixture of charcoal and animal manure and was magical in its potency. Everything we put out in that dirt would grow wildly like jack in the beanstalk. There was an old rotted-out windmill tower back where the barn had been. A tree had grown up attached to the windmill tower and intertwined into it.

That winter I cooked all kinds of good beans on that wood burning stove. Beans and bread like to simmer and it gives you an excuse to hang by the stove. My life was filled with basic chores. I had to go to bed real early at night. The opportunity to chop wood and haul a lot of water presented itself all day long in the dark ages. The house had a system of gutters going around the edge of the roof and these conducted rain down into a deep cylindrical well—the cistern. The old black folks who used to live there before, used to drink that rainwater. But that was before pollution. Now not even the spleen of City-boy Man, could handle rain. For drinking water there was a 7500 gallon galvanized steel water tank—with the proper bottom for drinking water—set upon a raised platform of interlocking rail road ties. Gregory had installed it. A Travis county service trucked the water out for twenty-six dollars a load. It was cheaper than plumbing. The out, of the house, was about fifty yards along a path toward the back and had a little half moon on the door.

Sometimes it got to be so alone out there that it was a big thrill just to sit on the front porch and watch the five-engined, ninety-five-car, freight train stretching across the valley floor—like a line snaking across the horizon way off in the distance—where the miles and miles of miles and miles came together and joined up with the endless blue of the Texas sky. From where I sat in a faded metal lawn chair with my feet up on the porch rail, it was too far away to hear it groaning and shuddering. Once I managed to go as long as two weeks without seeing another human being. Then I thought I had finally escaped the city.

I was happy leading this simple existence, writing, meditating, gardening and doing tai chi. The months moved on into spring. I was really broke and needed the garden for food and became a vegetarian.

It was really something to be doing tai chi in that flat land where all the crops had been cut down and nothing had started to grow yet. It made a standing man feel like the tallest thing around. Time got slowed way down to a glacier's pace, to a plate's pace and you could almost feel the land moving up from the Gulf of Mexico and merging with the prairie coming down through the middle of America. You could just feel the land itself, where these coastal plains that the farm was on, met up with the hill country in the western horizon. There the land turned west and rose up and became the high plains on its way up to becoming the Rockies.

When I'd have to walk into Manor, which was about 5 miles away by road, and probably 3 or 4 cutting across fields, I would usually stick to the roads. It is unwise to cut across fields in Texas. Redneck farmers will shoot you for trespassing. There weren't very stringent gun laws back then and the rednecks were always looking for an excuse to commit legalized murder. But the daily life of the small time farmer during the days of sprouting small plants in isolation on the farm precipitated boredom and after the rare spring shower I would venture into their fields to look for psilocybin mushrooms growing on cow shit. It turns out that these flatland cows around Manor weren't like the old world cows of the German farmers in the hill country outside of San Marcos where you could find *hongos hallucinentes*. These flatland cows were fed such large quantities of drugs that they became unmotivated and would mill around in gangs, hang out in packs in the shadows, with cigarettes hanging out of their mouths, wearing leather jackets. They were so full of antibiotics that mushrooms couldn't grow on the cow's shit. In the hill country you could find psilocybin mushrooms growing out of cow pies after a spring rain. Stumbling across a spray of *cubensis* was like finding the pot of gold at the end of the rainbow. Me and my friends would bring a canteen of water to wash and eat the mushrooms right out in the field, because the mushrooms showed you the way to other mushrooms.

The big ranchers in the flatland prairie around Manor poured all kinds of artificial fertilizer and bug sprays on their crops. The really big operations had their own galvanized tin silos full of the stuff and multiple sheds and garages for all their equipment. It was either rich white ranchers or poor rural blacks who lived out here. I didn't mix into either culture. I walked into Manor knowing that I didn't have a thing in the world in common with these people.

I thought about how the West was lost. What would have happened if the old guys in the calvary had known about marijuana. They did actually, called it goof butt, a hip term back then. What if, when they got off duty they had gone out behind the corral and smoked some goof butt. What if the mostly white calvary had gotten off their high horses and smoked some weed with the Indians. And maybe some of the Mexicans who smoked it too had come over and maybe some of the men and women got naked and jumped into an irrigation ditch together to cool off in the sweltering heat. That would really have been something, wouldn't it? They might have accepted each other. And what if some newly freed Negro slaves who now owned property in the area had come over too, and brought out some of that good gage and some bodacious barbecue and they all had a picnic. That would have really fixed things wouldn't it? They would have created a whole new alternative history for America. We would have had a different history in which the white men were able to see from the perspective of the Indians, could travel into the underworld of their spirits and have visions and come back again, able to integrate into their rational science the unfolding harmony of nature. Basically the Indian could have taught the white man how to live within his bio-niche and about community, and the white man could have brought the Indian out of the third world into the world of microchips and monoclonal antibody technology. Better yet, they two could have developed a really useful, spiritual technology. That would really have been something, wouldn't it?

5

THE BOOK OF BREEDING

The first time I saw the book of breeding was at Gregory's house in Austin. He seemed to be always writing in it.

Gregory was a secretive, taciturn fellow. Like me a loner and a recluse. When I came into town or was on my way out we'd meet and hang out in Greg's big back room with his two Doberman dogs, smoking pot and talking about growing, occasionally even cooking a meal together on the industrial strength stove in his kitchen. Gregory kept his little black science lab notebook by his bed into which he occasionally entered a note about the taste and the high of the smoke.

Gregory seemed to live mostly in that one big back room which took up the whole back of his house. He always came in and went out of the back door, crossing his backyard to the gate, then going across the alley to where he parked his car under a tree.

Greg took me into his confidence. "Since we're partners, I guess I'll have to trust you." He led me down the hall, which was an obstacle course of stacks of wood and drop lights and other carpentry stuff and he opened a tightly sealed door. It made a fethaah sound as he pushed it in.

I was hit full in the face by a blast of hot white light and an overpowering smell of skunk quickly infusing the air and stinking to high heaven. It almost made me nauseous. I felt sweaty. Nothing in my experience prepared me for what I saw as my eyes adjusted to the light. He led me into a windowless bedroom, where I saw a long table completely covered with plants under big metallic lights suspended from the ceiling with a rope and pulley system. Any outside windows had been paneled off. He had covered the walls with aluminum foil to reflect the light. A fan blew back and forth sending gentle waves into a sea of green plants. We had to be careful where we stepped because across the floor snaked cables and black plastic tubing.

"Jesus," I said reacting to the smell, waving my hand in front of my nose.

"Pretty strong isn't it." he said. "I usually have to take a shower after I work in here. Lucky it is pretty well automated and I don't have to come in here that much."

He began to move around pointing out things. "The lights are 600 watt sodium lamps, on timers, 12 hours on and 12 hours off.

"Now this is what you call intensive gardening. This here is kind of like a production nursery. "

I hate to admit it but this jungle of dark, serrated leaves was the first time I had ever actually seen marijuana growing.

He walked around showing it off, pointing at the pipes and things, "This network of plastic pipes supplies the plants with water. That big tank there has carbon dioxide, cause the plants need it." He pointed at the top of the table, "There's a heater in their to keep their little roots toasty at night."

Seeing how I was kind of shocked and almost on the verge of gasping for air he said, "Yea this is that stinky ole skunk weed that they grow in California, they've got it worked out so that it really produces in a hurry. I can get a crop three times a year. I've got a regular little sweat shop here don't I."

He shook his head in dismay. "I had to go to unbelievable trouble to set of this system of fans and ducts to pull the air out of these rooms and move it up the chimney. Luckily this house has a really high chimney, because it must be like a winter fire going on up that flue there."

"Did you ever see plants that looked more pleased, he said, walking around touching them. "I give them everything they want, carbon dioxide, fertilizer (and this stuff is not all that organic), hot bright lights.

"I mainly grow these plants inside to develop the seeds. You never can be too careful."

Greg had partitioned off two big rooms and several closets in the rest of his house and turned it into a seed incubation factory.
"I've got it down to a science," he said. "I can grow about 3 crops a year, and have separate rooms, and closets, some just for growing seed stock. Strongest weed I ever grew was some I grew in that mirror-lined closet under the stairs."
He grew multiple varieties, and prided himself on developing "a very high grade, fruity pot. Everybody loves it."

In another room large green pickle buckets of potting soil had been set out under immensely bright lights; in another room he had a hydroponics system, trays and plastics and the plants stuck in rockwool. There was ducting for forced air. His whole house was a secret, intensive, pot garden—inside—under lights.

To me the plants looked nice enough; I didn't know what I was looking at — I couldn't tell a male from a female. This lack of knowledge was embarrassing to me and it made me defensive around Gregory. Sinsimilla was just starting to catch on then. All the weed most people in my generation had ever seen was the "gold" weed that came in chunks, which we thought was just fine. A pound was a little less than half a kilo brick that came wrapped in a Mexican newspaper. A lid had to be broken off of that. When you broke open a brick it emitted a smell that was a mixture of barnyard straw and marijuana. A good part of the brick was sticks and stems and seeds, and there was often a dirt clod or two in it, no doubt to add to the weight. It was all an indiscernible lump, hard to see what was leaf and what was flower, and yet one associated a thrill with that smell.

But then a couple of years ago the United States authorities began working with the Mexican Government to spray Mexican marijuana fields with the herbicide paraquat, and this got everyone in the user community very worried about the safety of imported marijuana. It is what really started off the home freedom garden movement eventually making the domestic agriculture product America's most valuable crop.

Now, of course, most people are much more sophisticated and can speak knowledgeably of the bouquet, and the distinction between the musky heavy smell of indica and the light invigorating smell of sativa. We know that the "gold" is partly due to mildew and rot and that well-handled weed is green with fiery little tendrils that you can see and smell — not all crushed up. Well-cured weed has the right moisture content: not over dried to dust nor too wet as to be unsmokable.

The seeds that he kept in little vials with black tops were cross correlated to more elaborate detail cribbed in a neat hand on 3 x 5 cards and stored in a metal recipe box. Each card had information transcribed from the notebooks about the aroma of the bud—whether it was musty or pungent or minty; what the bud looked like; what kind of shape it was in; how it had been handled; how the smoke tasted.

"I've got a scale of numbers from one to ten of how stoned a particular smoke makes me feel," Greg said. "I'm on the quest for a marijuana of character."

When Gregory came out to the land it was to do work. He was very capable and officious. He was always directing everything. He walked around like he owned the place. Gregory and I planted the germinated seeds in tall grapefruit juice cans full of the magical barn dirt. Under Greg's direction he and I had been drinking Texsun Pink grapefruit juice out of the tall cans.

"These cans are perfect," he said. "Drink juice all winter, stay healthy, leave the can out in the rain for rust is good for the plants. Puts iron in their soul."

We used a nail to make a neat even ring of 4 or 5 holes around the can at about 2 inches from the bottom. This was so there would always be a reservoir of water in the bottom of the can, in case the plant had to go a long time unattended. It was a kind of hydroponics.

Gregory was especially keen to see that each can was properly labeled. He wanted to know whether it was a hybrid or what strain it was. So he had tags with a big number on them, the same number from the tray of germinating seeds. These tags had even been laminated with clear hard plastic to protect them from the elements. They were tied to the cans by a wire that went in one of the drainage holes and out the other. This was done before they even put the dirt into the cans.

"The main thing is that we keep this number going all the way through the process," said Greg. "That is the key."

He looked over at me and with his usual condescending air snarled, "You got your book?"

"Yeah," I said, defiant and sullen.

"Well get it."

"Yes sir, aye, aye, sir." I said, doing a step'n'fetchit number.

I chafed under Greg's controlling attitude. Greg was nearly always crotchety and impatient, but he was also the expert. You had to respect his ideas and unlike me, Greg had a fierce work ethic.

Greg picked up my mood and softened a bit. "You've got to keep a book. That way you can double check on me. We've got to keep track of the breeding. It's gonna get really complicated. We're gonna be doing a lot of experiments in breeding out here. And cloning. And espalier."

I opened my book to a page. We both looked at it. It was nearly blank. "Well, at least I've entered the name of the hybrid," I said apologetically

"You can copy stuff out of my book," said Greg. "Be sure to write down the date when we put these in to the ground. We want to keep track of how long it takes them to bloom."

We carried the cans out to the hot box nursery we had built in open yard behind the house. Greg and I had built three rows of long hot boxes, maybe 15 feet long. They were covered with glass window panes. We set the planted cans out into the hot boxes.

Greg picked up one of the tags on the cans. "See...look. For example this one here, number 18. It says these seeds are c. sativa Mexico crossed with C sativa Thai.

"This one shouldn't take forever to flower," he said. "The Thai's usually take forever, but crossing it with the Mexican will make if flower sooner. But there might be something bad about these seeds, and we have to find out about it."

"What else goes into the book?" I asked.

"Well number 1 is the quality of the stone. I would like that good healthy stone, that doesn't leave you groggy."

"Yeah, me too."

"And when they do flower we want them to grow big flowers."

"Yeah, that'd be nice. Big flowers."

"And we don't want them to take until December to do it," Greg said. "It would be nice if it didn't take forever in the fields. It's going to get weird out here, I tend to get really paranoid. And it would be nice if it tasted good and had a good smell."

And as an afterthought he added "It would be nice if it was easy to dry and cure and store. And also it's got to make viable seeds to propagate itself."

"Damn, you don't want much. Do you."

"Nothing less will do," said Greg. "Basically, what we are doing is planting hybrids. That F1 hybrid generation is for sure at least going to meet our number one criterion and that is it has a good stone. I'd be happy if we got that, but it would be nice to get plants that are able to select for at least one of these other good attributes from their parents."

For some reason I started calling the soft rounded almost succulent first leaves of the marijuana plants Jefferson airplanes. They looked like funny little cartoon airplanes to me trying to take off from the earth, but still attached on their little wire like stems. I kept this appellation to myself, of course, for fear Gregory would scoff at me.

6

THE WILD AND GENTLE DOG

"You need to get a dog out here." Gregory said one day. "In the country, you can tell a lot about a place by the kind of dog an owner puts out."

Gregory had two pedigreed Dobermans that he kept at his house in Austin. He rarely brought them out to the farm because he didn't want them to get dirty or get ticks on them. He was very proud that the male was the progeny of Corgedor de Diablo, the Devil Chaser.

"Have you seen that place down the road into Manor with the two Dobermans out front?" Greg asked.

"You mean the one where the owner has a cyclone fence topped by three strands of barbed wire and behind it two fast moving snarling Dobermans whose ears have been shaved to a point to make them look like devil dogs?" I asked.

"Yeah. That one," Greg said, looking at me quizzically.

"What do those dogs tell you about that place?" I asked.

"It tells me, don't go in there!" Greg laughed.

"That's for damn sure," I said. "The owner must have one hell of a large territorial imperative."

"Uh, what?"

"He's got to have a lot of space around him."

"That place says to me: Don't go in there!" Greg reiterated.

"Yeah that's true," I said. "But it really draws a lot of attention to itself. It almost says, 'I've got a speed lab in here', or something like that."

"Well, yeah, maybe you're right." Greg said, "Anyway, you need to get a dog out here."

Yes, a dog. I began looking for a dog. As luck would have it, around about that time, I got a job. At Juvenile Hall. It was from one of the co-workers at Juvie that I got my dog, Butch.

Yes, a marijuana farmer becoming a custodian of today's errant youth. The whole situation shimmered in a kind of sick irony that created a pervasive watchful paranoia. It seems all my life I have had to stir up a bunch of cognitive dissonance in order to feel normal. Cognitive Dissonance, CD, was another kind of drug for me.

Even in the dark ages, one had to hitchhike back and forth into town to get some money to pay rent and incidentals. The position at the Travis County Juvenile Home was obtained through the advocacy of a friend. Texas was one of the last places that still arrested and detained runaways. I was given the midnight to morning shift.

It was quite a change going from the country to the town. The highway into Austin was 1000 yards to the north of my back door (through dense growth, so you couldn't go that way). I would walk out the quarter mile driveway to a rural road; turn left; walk another half mile up the road to the highway. There I would stick out my thumb to start hitchhiking into Austin.

The highway there was like a berm or a levy above the flat land. To the east, west, and south, you saw just the prairie, no trees for miles, just endless fields of sorghum and wheat. It was like going from pre-industrial revolution rural poverty to the urban hum. I caught rides with all kinds of people, guys in the military, students, rednecks—but never any women. They'd drive talking or not talking, past the flat land expanding out in a neat patchwork of fields all segmented off by fences to the horizon. In the fields were huge rolls of alfalfa all rolled in bundles like giant shredded wheat. We drove past quarries, and little townships, gas stations and cafes, past little farm houses in the shade of trees, coming into the denser neighbor-hoods, getting denser and denser until we were in the tree lined avenues of Austin. There I could catch a free, university shuttle bus. The juvenile hall was all the way out Congress avenue on the other side of Austin. It took two bus rides, one into campus and one out.

The job was okay because it let me be a substitute and I didn't have to really belong to anything. I so needed this job that I even consented to wearing a wig to cover my long hair in order to get it. As I said, this, going under cover into the heart of the oppressor's territory, seemed to satisfy some kind of terrible need I had in my make-up for cognitive dissonance. I had long hair down to my shoulders, which I had to keep pinned up under a wig in order to hold down this job. I actually believed it would be good for some of these boys to be around a white guy who wasn't an oppressive authority figure. The wig got knocked off one time when I got hit a glancing blow by a basket ball thrown by one of the juvies. It knocked the wig off the top of my head and my long hair did come tumbling down in front of god and all those juvenile delinquensts.

They were shocked and delighted at this moment of truth.

I have often wondered why it is necessary for me to have a lot of cognitive dissonance in my mind. I seemed to thrived on it. I prided myself in being able to balance antipathic lifestyles and the rural hippie pot farmer on the one hand and urban social worker on the other were about as opposite as I could imagine. I suppose it is another way of keeping yourself sedated.

Yes, a dog. It was one of my co-workers at Juvenile Hall, who had some border collies he needed to find homes for. This man had been a cop and now was a preacher. He lived out in the country. I didn't like the man, a Baptist preacher who was sure he had been given the power by God almighty to smite the unrighteous. He had high blood pressure that made his face get all red and pocky and made his eyes bug out. He was sadistic and threatening to the juveniles. He would slap and threaten the juvenile delinquents. Some of whom were brawny as timber jacks and brainy as flapjacks. Still they were young and didn't deserve to be treated like that, unless necessary. It gave me a stomach ache to work a shift with him.

The preacher/cop was fond of telling the boys what would happen to them if they were sent to jail or prison. "The men up there are gonna commit all kinda awful sex acts on your body," he would say in a gloating, jeering way.

I borrowed a car and went out to his place in the country to pick out a dog. The preacher/cop eyed my long hair. I thought he was going to leap on me at any moment. As I looked over the litter, the fat little gargoyle began to rail against the Miranda warning, his face getting more and more demon like.

"That's why I quit the police force," he said.

"After they got the Miranda warning you just couldn't do your job any more. It was the worst thing to ever happen to law enforcement."

The man had one beautiful border collie, a black and white and fiery orange one that had already been named Butch. I looked at Butch and Butch looked at me, our eyes locked, and the dog communicated with me saying: 'O.K. I'm going with you.'

I took the dog real quick into my arms, put me into a box on the floor of the car, and took off.

Butch was a puppy that had never been to the city. He grew fast and within a couple of weeks I took him into Austin for his shots. Butch was freaked out at all the confusion of cars and roads. Funny and intelligent and full of life, Butch grew up there on the farm with me. Butch developed his instincts and his instincts were those of a sheep dog. He didn't pay much attention to cows when we went for walks, but Butch liked to chase sheep. We had to be cool though, because there were some mean white redneck ranchers in the area and they would just as soon shoot a dog messing with their stock.

Catman had become a dog man.

7

HEAD IN THE CLOUDS

Now in Texas, one thing there is plenty of, is sky and I had always enjoyed looking at the clouds. I had always been a kind of head in the clouds sort of guy. So out on the land, when the routine daily life of the small time isolated farmer during the early part of the growing season left one with plenty of time to sit on the porch and just watch the clouds changing shapes, I was able to raise sky watching to the status of at least a hobby, if not a religion.

The land is so flat on the prairie that on a good day, when there is a lot of turbulence, you can see enough of the sky at a time to see whole landscapes of river valleys bordered by hills, in the sky. Of course being under it is like a fish who has never been out of water wondering about the world above, but I was able to fill in with my imagination what these landscapes of the air looked like by recalling the view from airplane flights in memory. The resulting relativistic composite was free of the quantum uncertainty limitation of the airplane moving so fast through the sky while looking through a very small porthole because in a turbulent day on the farm, you are sitting still and it is sailing over you pretty fast. Some days there were heads one-hundred times the size of Mount Rushmore floating across the continent to give me a nod as they went skirting by—only to dissolve into an enormous bird or a fish.

On the porch, I would sit in this old, faded-orange, steel lawn chair and then lean way back balancing myself by putting my feet up on the rail. I'd look off into the horizon over mowed fields as far as the eye could see to where the fields just seemed to get longer and longer as the demarcations of their fences dissolved into the endless blue of the Texas sky.

Then one day while wondering about the relationship between the world above and the world below, I realized that in order to really "see" clouds you have to be able to look through the eyes of analogy and metaphor because when you look at the sky you can't see the forest for the trees! Clouds are air trees, and the reason why you can't see the trunks of the cloud trees is because the trunks are invisible *thermals* rising up off the hills and mountains, shimmering up off hot roads, roof tops, and cars, even dark green bushes. Anything that warms up faster than the other things around it. Both clouds and trees have mechanisms for sucking up moisture, distributing it around within themselves and conducting exotranspiration. It's just that clouds do it much faster. I tried to see with my imagination, the invisible thermals rising off the road, or houses or the town. Rooftops, for example. I'd imagine thermal bubbles rising out of the top of my house. They are bent and swaying like the streams of bubbles that rise in boiling water. Hours would go by without my noticing. No one has that kind of time to waste anymore.

On turbulent, cloud-filled days, I'd spend a lot of time just staring off into space surveying and doing cartography trying to picture this invisible landscape in the sky. I called this activity a kind of aeoliography of the air or aeoliology. I had invented a new science.

I knew these thermals rose up through layers of air stacked like pads and sheets and blankets on a bed, except these layers were on a very unmade bed, creating a geography of the air: the hills, the valleys, the river channels, the deep swirling pools. I knew the thermals were like the bubbles rising in boiling water that popped and went splat—like pabulum being flicked up onto the ceiling by an infant god testing out the laws of gravity—when they hit a layer that was of the same temperature. I knew the topography up there also moved rapidly in waves, the way the wind rifles trees and moves through fields of wheat down here, except at least the trees down here are rooted and can't go floating off.

I would have liked to be able to have an animated conversation with somebody about this analogy. I could see myself saying, "It's just that clouds take up moisture a lot faster than trees. The filaments of a cloud's tissues are its branches."

Yeah. Right.

Sometimes, when I was stoned, a marvelous thing would occur. The porch rail against which I was pressing my feet while I was leaning back in the chair would become a ledge I was standing on. And the chair would become the sheer wall of a cliff I was pressing my back into, or a skyscraper building upon whose upper ledge I had crawled out onto through a window. Sometimes it was so real I would get scared from the exposure and press my back further into the chair as if I were inching along a narrow ledge high up on a precipitous mountain cliff having to keep my back to the wall for dear life or fall to my death in the valley miles below. At first it was like looking at this great gigantic chessboard and these heads came drifting across the continent and moved over the grid of fields. And then it would be like these parts of the world, the mountains, and roads, and cars down below are dreaming or wishing they could be free to drift along over the continent and sail on the laughing wind. It was like the clouds were the dreams of the landscape percolating up in the form of invisible thermal wish bubbles.

Truly I was looking over the rim of the world into what that hot wearing sky really was. Then, suddenly, an enormous sphinx sitting proudly with its head held high staring endlessly would seem to be looking at sea horses rising and falling close by. There I would be with my feet propped up on the porch rail but truly believing I was on the edge of a cliff desperately trying not to loose my balance and fall into these swirling depths below. I would be sweating it out on the brink, as if it were real—at risk—in my sunglasses.

As if this were not enough, I'd conduct the same experiment while eating magic mushrooms. The results were an order of magnitude more thrilling and moving. They'd make me feel like I was a giant helium-filled balloon. I'd slip my moorings and float like a great big head over the landscape becoming part of it. My head was one of the clouds floating across the continent too. It was like strolling among the clouds.

When I got a ride in a *real* hot air balloon it was a big thrill of a different kind. It was Easter Sunday and I was sitting on the porch with Butch and hadn't seen a soul for nearly two weeks and some balloonists floated over. What a sight, these giant multicolored orbs drifting through the morning sky. Two balloons landed close together in the big mowed field just below my house. Butch and I went down to investigate. I got the idea of bringing some Cokes down to them, in hopes that they might offer to give him a little ride and in any case just to look at their fantastic flying machines.

They were mighty glad to get the cans of Coke and they did offer to take him up. I clamored into the lightweight wicker and aluminum basket which was outfitted with ballast bags and all kinds of straps. The balloonist turned a lever and the heater shot a flame six feet long into the heart of the bag and the balloon began to struggle up into the sky.

"We're taking off," the balloonist said.

"Bye, bye Butch." I said.

My wild and gentle dog, my shadow and medicine dog companion, looked strangely at me as I rose into the air. Even though I was belted in I held on for dear life. The tremendous red and orange ovaloid orb lifted the little wicker basket one thousand feet into the air and though I was practically pissing in my pants with fear I was also giddy and light-headed with delight.

The balloon trip was really beautiful and it gave him a useful perspective on aeoliology, but it was a totally clear day and they didn't go up that high, so I didn't get to study clouds up close.

When I got back I thought: somebody ought to do a study of the mound builders. Their shamans must have been able to take the mushroom and let a sensate projection of themselves float into the air and get high up above the land so they could design their great mounds. Yes, those mounds are probably not only icons to the Indian's religion but also testimony of a spiritual technology that included astral projection.

8

LOAFERS OF THE KANDINSKY SOUND MUSEUM

I took the opportunity while at the farm to become a loafer. Not the kind of loafer you see hanging out in the middle of the day, although I have done my share of that too, but the kind of loafer they mean when they refer to people who listen in to the VLF band (Very Low Frequency) on your radio dial. A loafer is also what they call these long, low-frequency radio waves. These waves fall in the audio range and go below the edge of human hearing. Some people say they go down into the realm of brain waves, into the unconscious.

VLF is a kind of natural radio, caused mainly by lightning but also magnetic solar storms hitting the atmosphere and geophysical activity of the plates floating around on the molten plasma core banging into each other scraping past each other. These long waves with their low frequencies pass through water and the earth quite easily and just go lobbing along bouncing back and forth between the earth and the sky and either pass through your body or are reflected away like water off a duck's back. But they can be picked up with a very big antenna. In particular, the wire fence around a ranch makes an excellent antenna.

I decided that it was so quiet out there on the prairie and so far from interference that it might be a good idea to hunt up some of this natural radio. So I brought out this old surplus Model TCX-31 radio, which was, in its day during the W.W.II, the highest form of radio technology. I first got introduced to collecting atmospherics, as they are called, by a teacher I was a TA for. They called him Ham not only because he was an amateur radio operator and buff, but he was a big, bearded, meaty sort of guy—a strange bird, brilliant and wonderful, a fantastic foolly-bear of man. Ham had lovingly maintained this marvelous old tube radio and trained me how to do it before giving it to me.

I had been touched by the gift. I didn't know why Ham had given me such an elegant instrument, but suspected it was out of gratitude for the way I looked out after him, running interference for him between the real world of students and the pure world of divine nature seen in abstract thought that Ham most liked to inhabit. Ham was a very lost in the ozone techie, techie sort of guy, shuffling down the hollowed halls of the junior college, lost in thought. He always wore the same outfit: flannel shirt and shapeless olive drab army fatigues.

Ham had somehow managed to rent a great old Austin Victorian

40

house in a nice neighborhood even on the junior college salary. The grounds fairly bristled with antennas. His poor wife —it was like a rabbit warren inside. You moved among tables of radios and electronic gear. Ham was always lurking around surplus lots, picking up incredible buys on instruments. He had two or three of every radio, which he kept around for parts. He loved working on them.

"It's like performing brain surgery." He'd say. "A very delicate operation to tune the super heterodyning system in these old World War II radios.

"You have to tune the line of transformer stages in amongst the tubes and high-precision military components with a plastic screwdriver in order not to contribute to the ferocapacitance and mess up the signal."

Ham was a teacher from the old school. He felt hurt and took it personally when any of his students didn't learn. Even worse was how shocked and disappointed he became when it came out, with irrefutable evidence, that there was wide spread cheating going on in his classroom. The students cheated all the time because he was always so distracted he didn't notice. I was afraid Ham might go into cardiac arrest. The absent minded professor was such a sensitive do-gooder that it made me want to protect one such as he who was just totally without a bit of street sense. All the students made fun of him behind his back. Many of the students were the privileged sons and daughters of rich Arabian oilionairs.

Ham was an experimentalist, always trying to get people to experience the natural phenomena directly instead of discussing equations all the time. My own education had been so nominalist and abstract it left me with a real hunger to feel something real. I wanted to become a man of knowledge and it was mainly because of Ham that I hung out there at that school and worked for such a measly little sum.

Ham built most of the experiments for the physics department. He built a Van De Graff generator and a huge Tesla coil. It was like something out of a Frankenstein movie, it threw a long blue arcing spark across its antipodes. Ham was a devotee of Tesla.

"Tesla showed how the earth is a huge capacitor," he'd say, "the sky above is one plate and the earth below is another. And the atmosphere in between is dielectric. It stores charges and they are moved around by the wind, and when they get built up too high there is a discharge of lightning. Tesla started to build a giant coil and use it to tickle the atmosphere at its resonate frequency. He wanted to resonate this whole atmosphere so he could broadcast energy!"

Ham built wave guides, out of long parallel rods that ran the length of the lab. He had an experiment where you could light little fluorescent bulbs just by moving them around over the rods. The lights would grow brighter and dimmer according to the shape of the radio energy which got more intense at nodes.

One thing I will never forget is the look on Ham's face one day when they were showing the class a film about the Crab Nebula, which is the remnant of a super nova—an exploding galaxy— millions of light years away. It had first been noticed from the earth as a bright light dominating the heavens for days in 1054. Ham looked long and wistfully at the beautiful colored explosion expand- ing outward against the background field of stars. His eyes scanned the radio sky looking for lonely stars that perhaps had planets orbiting around them in which there were people just like him who could communicate through the dimension of mind, one archetype to another outside of time. Ham's face became sad, pensive. I thought my teacher might start crying in front of the classroom.

Ham said, "When I look at this gigantic explosion I think about the millions of beings that died in this explosion." I was shocked to hear the man of science admitting his belief in extraterrestrials.

But the most far-out thing Ham did was to present his noise collection, what he called his Noise Museum. He pursued noise relentlessly. In addition to being an amateur radio expert he was also an audiophile and he'd bring his great big 10-inch reel-to-reel to the lecture, set it down there on the big black slab of a lab table where it looked like some whirly-eyed nerd brain with glasses.

There were 25 or 30 in the class, mostly male sitting on stools at the lab tables. Ham called roll because he had been nailed and harassed so much by the administration, that he now made it a point to be a stickler for detail.

"Aboulijhana."

"Here."

"Dong."

"Uh huh."

"Salamani."

"Yep."

Most of the students seemed to be the sons of Iranian magnates wearing Rolex watches which cost more than a teacher's monthly salary. It galled me that these students drove BMWs to this poor little junior college campus, while I rode the shuttlebus. They were just here to get their physics out of the way at the junior college because it was easier than at the university. They didn't realize what a great opportunity it was to study with this man.

"Here, let me play it for you," Ham said, as he pressed on the big relay controller button which made a resounding cathunk as it activated the reel to reel. "I'm going to take you on a sound tour of the earth and sky."

The class was immediately assailed with the most amazing cacophony of clicks, pops and tweaks—static, known as spherics. There were sounds like air escaping from a punctured tire and swishes like a whip being snapped through the air. The students all looked at each other and rolled their eyes, shifted uncomfortably in their seats.

I loved it. I had first heard about spherics in a Thomas Pynchon novel in the '60s. In fact, it was that novel which had been so instrumental in turning me from literature to physics.

Ham started with the whistler. The class heard a click and then the very pure gliding tones. It sounded like "piou" a sound whose tone decreased through the complete tonal scale and ended with the deepest audible sounds before disappearing into the background noise.

"This one—that one—right there," Ham said, "is the famous whistler. See, first you get the click and then the associated whistler. The click is the lightning.

"Most of the noise we hear on the radio is from lightning storms. At any given time there are thousands of storms going on all over the earth."

"And each stroke of lightning is about 250 million volts, which is way more wattage than any radio station, but it's only for a very short time. It's fun to try and figure out how far away the storm is and in what direction."

Ham started to draw, with white chalk on the black board, the butterfly-shaped magnetic dipole of the earth. The great looping arches of magnetic field lines came out of the north pole, curved back around in larger and larger perimeters around the earth and re-entered the world by the south pole. Soon the earth looked like it had these huge Dumbo ears or like it had butterfly wings.

"A lightning bolt dumps radio energy into the atmosphere," Ham would begin, "where it glides along a magnetic field line — sometimes out of the ionosphere into black space — into the opposite hemisphere and back again. That is a one hop whistler. It *can* bounce back and forth several times.

"Here. Listen. Here is a two-hop whistler."

He drew graphs of the whistler's time and frequency curves on the black board, as well as the spreading crawl of its dispersion. "And along the way the radio signal is dispersed."

Ham was taking the class on a fascinating journey, a tour of the atmosphere, the ionosphere, and the magnetosphere. They were in the jungle of the universe full of strange sounds and mathematical wildlife, relating the calls emitted by these physical phenomena to their causes. Instead of gun and camera they had radio receiver and sound tapes. My mind slipped into gear. It was incredible.

Ham would go into some of the lore. He was like an old hand weaving war stories out on the Veldt as if he had been there. "The way these whistlers were first discovered was during the 1st World War. They wanted to overhear enemy telephone conversations. Because there was poor insulation, the conversation would be induced into the ground near the phone cables, and the engineers would pick up these conversations by sticking metallic probes into the ground at points several hundred yards apart, just like those wave guides we made. The probes were connected to the amplifier which in turn was connected to the telephone.

"They were called whistlers by telegraph operators trying to pick up secret Axis code transmissions in the trenches of World War I. They would hear these sounds flying by, and it snuck up on you. They thought it was like a bullet flying by and it was extremely unnerving.

"But enough of that, here's another spheric sound I'd like to show you." Here there would be a chorus of sonic chirping and barking-echo trains. "This one they call the dawn chorus, because it sounds like a multitude of birds waking up in the morning. These come in all kinds, hissers, risers and warblers.

"I want you to listen very carefully to this one because it gives us a picture of the varying density of the ionosphere. The ionosphere is like a skin around the world and it becomes thicker and thinner with day and night and gets blown out of shape by the solar wind. It's a plasma, a swirling swarm of electrons, and when a radio signal hits it, the signal gets bounced around inside the plasma like it is being reflected off of tiny mirrors. Then when the signal finally escapes and is coming back to us, it comes back at different times—a few milliseconds behind itself on different channels."

Then Ham would get a twinkle in his eye and riff off on one of his favorite metaphors. "It's like, ... try to imagine a whole heard of zebras running. Imagine them running into a thick stand of tall cane out on the pampas somewhere. It's as if the zebras could get strained as they ran through the canes." But all he'd get back were oppressed stares of thinly veiled disinterest. Nevertheless he'd carry on.

"What we are hearing," he said, "are the VLF emissions triggering one another in a harmonious chain reaction. That occurs when there are solar flares causing a rain of particles from inside the sun to stream down around our planet. This solar wind is what causes the northern lights. Chorusing is the acoustical analog of the aurora borealis!"

Ham would be telling us this while at the same time expanding on his drawing showing the solar wind coming from the lightside hitting on this butterfly magnetosphere, kind of bending it out of shape like a butterfly trying to fly into a head wind, and it has a long tail stretching out into the darkside.

Actually the sound was soothing, like raindrops on a tin roof. There is something beautiful about the randomness of the white noise, being shaped by all these lightning discharges and movement of the solar winds, and the magnetic fields and other plasma activity of the earth.

I found himself rooting for the whistler as the line snaked out from the swirling blue and white mists, punching through the shining plasma of the e-layer and threading its way along the curve of a magnetic field line through the clear blackness of space above the cloud shrouded earth to partake in the processes that formed the swirling constellation and then return to us emerging from a pale blue abstract sky.

It was indeed a noise museum. Ham was able to get them to see it the way he saw it, as a collection of colorful sounds hurtling through black space beyond the ionosphere and standing out against the texture of the background noise to loom into the view of our interpretation.

For some reason, maybe it was the abstract diagrams—the junior college had those old time blackboards and it was white chalk against a black board—and the diagrams would almost dissolve into an abstract painting, that I was reminded of Kandinsky's white-on-black sketches, with their harmonious forms and lines and great curving arches relating to a black and red sun. The shapes did have sounds, with descending whistlers, and ascending channel twists. The sounds diagrammed on the black board intermixed with fluffy blots of noise like chalk from an erased drawing. Kandinsky was around during the ascendancy of radio, and the splitting of the atom, and was really sensitive to that stuff. He put sand in some of his paintings so that they would have texture, and they looked all mottled and granulated, like the blots of muffled sounds that were coming out of the speakers. The crystals of sand break light up into its colors. The crystals in the radio break radio waves up into the voices and music coming in.

I thought of it as the Kandinsky Sound Museum. These abstract sounds like Kandinsky's paintings, required a lot of interpretation at first—the sound plus the diagrams and sometimes the equation.

In order to keep from boring the students catatonic, Ham would save the hard core discussions for a few of the TAs and other professors in his office.

"Of course that's understandable because..." he'd say and launch into a long concatenated reasoning process based upon attacking Maxwell's equations with divergence and curl to derive the difference between a whistler and a tweak. It was marvelous.

Ham had captured one spheric on tape that he couldn't understand or identify. He called it the Lion's Roar. And that's what it was. It was definitely the universe roaring outside that window. It reminded I of the Monster of the Id harnessed by the poor Crell in the movie Forbidden Planet. It was the one spheric that eluded Ham, although he was pretty sure it was underground nuclear testing.

Anyway, Ham just gave I the deluxe VLF receiver.

I knew the warm mornings in May and June would be especially good for picking up whistlers. I ran a very long antenna line from the fence to the receiver back at the house. (Gregory had had the electricity turned on.) I clipped this line onto the wire fence with a pair of alligator clips. But before I could jack in, me and Butch walked the 3-something miles of fence all around the place while the weeds were still not too tall, to make sure that there was no physical contact between the strands of fence shorting out the signal on their antenna, or that there was no part of the antenna touching ground.

I found that I was able to pick up many interesting sounds out there with such a large antenna. I was pulling in waves that are 11,000 miles long! They went a quarter way around the earth. It made him feel like a giant walking across the landscape. The waves are reflected off the under surface of the ionosphere and passed through my fence antenna into my VLF radio receiver and me and Gregory captured them into a tape recorder.

I thought that by capturing some of these sounds the way Ham did I could maybe make a contribution to physics. Like Ham I was not fit for working in the real world. And here was actually a frontier you could explore. You didn't need any license, it costs nothing, you didn't have to be part of a lab at some university and you are not buying into the commercial recording system and ego-based starmaker machinery. I was looking for something. I supposed it was just the universe underlying all reality. Natural radio was a way to pick up and stay in touch with that in a way.

What was the point? To feel like a giant walking over, better— flying over—the landscape? Looking at Kandinsky' abstract landscapes made me feel like I was soaring above little patchwork fields like some old time sorcerer. Being a part of the Loafer Landscape was like being in a Kandinsky synesthesia, flying above the white sky, flying above the white clouds, flying above the blue sky, surfing on the wind from big explosive sun spots, or sliding down the jagged edges of lightning, catching the curve of a magnetic field line, and riding the foam of the soft luminescent white noise of radio spectrum into the background.

Listening to VLF led me into the loafer landscape. When I got stoned out there and listened to it, really listened into this natural radio of our part of the universe, I'd start thinking, wondering. Wondering: what about Kandinsky? I would ask himself weird aesthetical questions like, "Is it more a Kandinsky universe than a Picasso universe?" I didn't know.

To Ham listening to this cacophony of sounds was like looking at the universe through a radio window at a cosmic drama unfolding in which the actors were energy lions that roared, mythopoeic choruses that soared and birdlike twittering machines embodying mathematical shapes.

I, too, wanted to create natural sound paintings to hang in the Kandinsky Memorial Sound Museum. People would come to feel these down inside their brain, as projections of the gigantic atmospheric, meteorological and geological forces moving throughout the earth amid a web of fields.

The Background Hisss
of Summer

9

A PLAGUE OF LOCUSTS ON THE LAND

The sun got higher and higher on the ecliptic and Butch and I began to welcome the warm days of spring and generally settled into life out there.

A great variety of plants: Hawaiians, Thais, Colombians and the Texas Tornado hybrid were growing in juice cans all under glass in the bedding boxes. Greg had shown me how to pinch them off. This means that after the main stem has got some side stems growing on it, you cut off the main stem by deftly pinching it off between your thumb and finger nails. This makes the plant spread out and become bushy.

"It makes it so that you don't get the one really big main top," said Greg "but you get several slightly smaller tops"

When the pot plants outgrew the bedding boxes, we started putting them out into the earth—into the barn dirt and in some of the animal stalls.

We decided to plant the main part of the patch where the corral and barn had been. This was all overgrown. From the house you got there by going along a path through the tall grass and weeds, then going through a wall of bushes. There was a stand of trees back there. Because of snakes and ticks, you wouldn't expect anybody to be just wandering around back there.

I set about digging holes in the rich brown barn dirt. The dirt where the corral and a barn had burnt down was the most wonderful dirt you could ever ask for. Moist, it was like angels' food cake; dark, it was like devils' food cake. Stick a pitchfork into it and a clump of magnificent dark, rich, well-aerated earth would hang on your fork. The plants were in for a treat. I carefully upturned the plants in their cans, then loosening the root ball with a pat like a doctor delivering a baby, I gently conveyed the cylindrical root ball into its prepared hole in the ground. Then to seat the plant, I knelt before it, and with his hands closed in a circle flat on the ground around the stem of plant, put my full weight on the root ball, sealing it well into its new home in the earth. To take the edge off the transplant shock we gave each new plant a christening with a big near full-gallon slurk of gnarly organic fish emulsion.

The charcoal in the dirt provided good drainage, the cow shit supplied organics and bacteria and the fish emulsion, the slow-acting organic fertilizer with micro nutrients. I also hauled a bunch of this around to my food garden in a wheel barrow. This too was a very large garden, as big as most people's front yards. In the zealotry of a being a beginning gardener I had planted a dozen tomato plants.

To water the plants in the garden and patch I had to pull up the water in 5 gallon pickle buckets lowered over a wheel and pulley system into underground resevoirs. This made an eerie creaking sound. I pulled many buckets from out of the dark cylindrical cistern by the house for my food garden and out of another huge under-ground reservoir, back behind the barn for the patch. This had been a reservoir for the stock in the old barn.

"The water in that back cistern is old and dead things have fallen into it," Greg said. This made the water too almost magical in its potency.

52

On the farm I wore white most of the time. I loved cotton. I wore expensive cotton stitched shirts which had a lace trellis of holes in the weave so that the air could move through. I bought the shirts second-hand for next to nothing at a haberdashery on Austin's east side. I wore a wide brim Panama hat blocked into a slouch. I got several pairs of white pants from the same place. I had to wash them often because the pull chain to the well got his hands dirty and gardening is just plain hard work in the dirt.

There was a plague of locusts that year because the Spring had been so dry and there was not enough rain to soak the land and keep down their larva. There were grasshoppers all over everywhere.

Gregory would be out there yelling at them in a crotchety old Texas voice.

"Git. Go on. Git! Git!!" he'd say, picking one off a branch and flinging it with a flick of his wrist.

"God damn these grasshoppers anyway."

Greg and I fell into a panic. The locusts did a tremendous amount of damage and we were afraid our whole crop would be wiped out. The locusts would stick whatever passes for teeth, into the plant stem and drag downwards like a plow gnawing and stripping off long strips of skin. They would jump on the little plants and break off branches with their weight. And it was getting so hot! Surely this is hell thought I, with these monstrous imps leaping and bounding all over the place.

Gregory and I were determined that this was going to be organic gardening so it was out of the question to spray. One of the main reasons why we had decided to grow a freedom garden was because the federal government was having the Mexicans and South Americans spray the herbicide paraquat on their weed and people in the States were getting sick on that stuff. We didn't know what we were going do to get rid of the locusts.

One day Gregory collected a bunch of the grasshoppers in a box. He put them into a large Osterizer, and punched BLEND, turning them into juice. I thought it was kind of gross. This he sprayed on one of the plants.

"Ooh, gross," I said.

"It'll wash off," Gregory said.

It didn't bother the locusts one bit. They carried on as though it wasn't even there. Even when Gregory sprayed it directly on them trying to drown them in it. They just waded through the liquid remains of their own tribe.

Ahh, the insects. Aren't they tenacious?

10

A COUNTRY GENTLEMAN COMMISSIONS A WORK OF ART

When next Ruth was out to the land, I was lamenting, "I've done everything I can think of that's organic, to get rid of these grasshoppers. They are jumping up on my little guys and breaking off limbs!"

Ruth and I were sitting out back on the patio under the tree drinking lemonade and smoking some of Gregory's finest. I liked smoking dope and talking about religion. Ruth was a very spiritual person, and we would always get into these weird spiritual conversations. This suited me because I was uncomfortable with my level of commitment to this relationship so spiritual conversations of a drug related nature seemed like safe enough area. I also kept the subject close to art and sculpture because that was her interest too. Except sometimes I might stir things up. When I told Ruth about Gregory grinding locusts into a slush and spraying it onto the plants, she was shocked and disgusted.

"I don't like what Gregory did at all," she said. "If I had been here that would not have happened."

"Yeah it was pretty gross." I said.

After a long an awkward pause she said: "When I was a little girl we had lots of crickets and...katydids.

"Katydids is what we called the cicadas, and fireflies and when I was a little girl I especially liked the cicadas. I would just fall down on the ground and just *look* at them. I was fascinated by their structure, how they were so angular and they were just all lines, very masculine, very different.

"And I loved the color of them."

"They are real hard edged," I said, "got that thrusty stick-like masculine hard edge."

"Yes and they looked very smart."

I laughed.

"They did. They have a very wise face," she said. "They really do. They are more human than any other insect. You know in their face, not in their body so much but in their face. And you know, the fact that they can jump and hop, and get away from you I think was something that attracted me, to them."

"Yeah," I said, enjoying her innocence.

For a moment I saw Ruth as herself, as she might have been as a little girl looking, getting down close on her hands and knees and looking at this insect in the face. It was almost as if I were this small child looking at her from the perspective of the insect, my small face looking at her large face with big gentle eyes. The insects can probably tell that young girls mean them no harm.

"But I would love to just lie down," she said, "and get close to one and just sort of ... talk, I loved, ... I always talked to ... to things when I was a kid. I love talking to whatever.

"I would never kill, I would just never kill an ant, I would walk around them. I could never understand how anybody could mash anything."

"But I would just lie down on the grass and you know, talk with ·the grasshoppers as long as I could. And sometimes it would go on for a long time."

"Wow." I said. "Yeah." We smiled at each other.

I thought I better make an attempt to go along with the drift of the conversation into talking about childhood. I am usually reticent and adverse to thinking in public when I am stoned because it makes me introspective but I tried to be playful, "What language would they be talking, then, these this incredible insect intelligence beings?"

"What language? Ruth asked, not quite sure, where the conversation was going.

"Well" I said, "they'd probably express themselves in a kind of Chinese idiomatic language. It would be a natural language like a stream of thrusty stick figures."

"Yeah, uh yeah," she laughed in a phantic way. "But yeah, I just really liked their shape. I can see their eyes and it's like they look like old men, you know they look like old men and uh, and I used to

56

connect or think about how they were like praying mantises which I mostly only saw when we went to this summer cottage for two weeks. I grew up in the city and there weren't too many in the city although sometimes I would see them on the side of a house or a porch.

"I didn't see too many of them but it was like so sacred when I did," she said.

"Were you particularly religious?" I asked.

"Me? I was...yea, I grew up pretty..."

"So you thought they were really praying," I interjected.

"I pretty much was very gullible," she continued, "and if someone told me something, like dragon flies..."

"O yea, bi-wingers," I added.

"Yeah," she continued, "I was told not to keep my mouth closed when they were around because they would sew your lips up!"

"Oh," I gasped, "how horrible." I had been told that same story.

"I was really afraid of them too," I said. "We called them darning needles."

"Yeah darning needles," she agreed.

"Well we just had to keep running around and talking," she continued. "It was OK as long as you didn't keep your mouth together so as soon as you saw them you had to like, scream and sing or run around and talk a lot."

"Wow, that's a pretty good strategy." I laughed.

I started feeling a kind of love for her, an affinity with her, for having been lied to as a child, for the world of belief that we lived in as children.

"It's interesting all these things connected to insects," Ruth said.

"Yeah, I can remember being on this porch and there was this preying mantis and my mother was saying, (I think my brother wanted to kill it) and she said 'You know, he's praying, he's praying for...the world.' Or whatever. And it looked like their hands were folded in prayer."

"Hmmm." I said, interested.

"Yeah, I don't know," she said. "They would be so still and stay for hours. People who are praying do that."

"Ah, I see, mediation." I said.

"Meditation, it was like meditation," she agreed.

Ruth looked wistful, like a big kid. "Yeah the grasshopper was my favorite insect when I was a kid, definitely."

"Hmmm," I agreed.

Then she had the bright idea. "Maybe that's what you should get here, a praying mantis on this farm. Maybe that might help with all you're trying to do here."

"Yeah, maybe we could get them to prey on the grasshoppers," I said. "I've done everything I can think of that's organic, to get rid of these grasshoppers."

"Maybe you should try praying," Ruth said, mock serious.

"Or some kind of animal sacrifice," I said, looking at the Bugle, raising and lowering my eyebrows at Ruth to tease her.

Bugle gave me an uncomfortable smile.

"Ohh, no you don't," she said, snatching up the dog into her arms and giving him a hug.

"Yess, but you might be right though," I said. "A more mystical approach. Why not."

"I am kind of appalled," I continued, "at what Gregory has done. Maybe it isn't too far off that we need to somehow fix it with Mother

Nature, even if she is giving us a beating. We need to make some kind of atonement. We have perhaps been abandoned, or been put way in the back of Her mind. Might not be a bad idea, to pray.

"Let's see. How would it work? What would the mechanism be?" I said musing aloud. "In order to appease the hunger of the grasshopper God, I must feed its ego. I must build a flattering image of him and pay homage to it."

Ruth looked suspicious.

I smiled at her.

She grinned as she lifted the bottle of Shiner.

Then the idea came to me.

"I've got it! I'll make an ICON of the grasshopper. And pray to it!"

I leapt up out of my chair.

"We'd need to invest the icon with our concentration and proper focus," I said.

I clasped my hands behind my back and started to stride in a stiff legged pitched forward duck-walk like some mad Groucho Marx - Professor Quackenbush pacing in front of my class making my eyebrows go. "We would need to work some kind of sympathetic magic...To get the totem of the grasshopper to...to intercede with the hoard. Yeah, like some kind of Trojan horse that they would accept."

"Yeah," she said, egging me on. "Ooh, I love it when you talk metaphysical like that."

"Yeah, a Trojan grasshopper!" I said. "One that passed through a wavering shifting mirage from our dimension into theirs."

I closed one eye and looked suspiciously over at Ruth to see if she was enjoying this. She was smiling, shaking her head and laughing at my folly. "Yes! What I need is a Trojan grasshopper."

Then I looked at Ruth straight. "What about it. You're a sculptor. You could make me one. Couldn't you?"

Because I was starting to have a little weed and starting to believe that a little money would be coming in behind it, I was beginning to hope that for the first time in my life I'd have a few bucks. It went to my head.

"I'll commission a work!" I exclaimed. "How much would it cost to have a small icon of the grasshopper made."

"O, I don't know," she said, drawing back in surprise, incredulous. Then she appeared to consider it.

"Look I don't have a lot of money," I said, "but I've got weed. Weed is worth money. Could you make me an icon if I gave you, say, half a pound?"

"Yeah," she said agreeing immediately.

I played the part puffing myself up. "I'm a country gentleman now. I can afford to be a patron of the arts. Could you do a sculpture for that?"

"You bet," she said, beaming.

"OK."

"And the first thing we'll need to do," she said, setting down her Shiner on the split log table, "is catch one to study."

"That'll be easy."

"We could put it in one of those Mason jars you've got in the kitchen," she suggested.

"All right! We can use one of those sprout lids for a top over it." I said.

We walked around to the front of the house, out to the edge of where the tall grass was cut back to. I just reached out my hand and gently plucked one off a tall reed and put it into a Mason jar.

11

SEX PATROL

"No! Gawd damn it!"

There was Gregory's slow, distinct, deliberate and denigrating drawl again.

"This here's the *male*, with these little pouches dangling down. *They* got the pollen in them."

Gregory had shown me how to tell the difference between the male and the female. Males have these raggedy looking little pouches hanging in clusters, like those balls in front of a pawn shop. Females have these tufts of sticky tendrils that start out white running milky clear in which to catch the pollen.

"Make sure you inspect the patch at least a couple of times a day," he ordered. Gregory directed either himself or me to be on sex patrol, assiduously inspecting each of the plants for early sex development in order to be offing the males.

"Be especially on the lookout for hermaphroditism," Gregory had said.

In the patch at the end of a hidden path we had planted by groups: Hawaiians, Thai, Mexican, Colombians, some hybrids. The giant Ganjas had been given even better quarters: little self-contained bungalows in the old animal pens. The plants that survived the onslaught of grasshoppers were struggling bravely, only to be scrutinized by — the sex patrol.

Because of all the locust damage, we didn't have to prune any of those inner limbs that you find on the lower internal parts of the plant. These are considered suckers, because they are hidden in the shade of the outer leaves. They had all been chewed off. Soon I was offing the early males by myself and it was then I started becoming my own authority.

•••

Another day Gregory said, "It worries me that we are getting such a large number of hermaphrodites. It might be that I have hybridized the seeds too much. I've checked the pH of the soil and that is the only reason I can come up with. In any case, pull them up."

Gregory was on personal terms with every plant in the patch. He'd walk through pointing out plants and talk about their origins. "This one, I got from a dealer friend of mine. It comes from the Congo. When my friend got this weed, it came tied up like a burrito, in a big leaf of elephant grass."

Greg pointed to one of the giant ganjas which was lounging in its own pen and said, "I got this giant ganja from a friend who was studying in the Dalai Lama's ashram in India. He was in some country hotel up there and noticed these marijuana plants growing outside his second story window! He said he just reached outside his hotel window and picked a bud off the tree. I have never had the room to grow them until now. They are supposed to have trunks as big around as a softball and grow something like 24 feet high. And it is real ganja!"

Gregory was really excited. He'd go around worrying out loud like a mother hen, wringing his hands going, "Man, I really want to grow this Ganja. We've got to give this one everything it wants. Those farmers in India have been growing ganja and developing this strain for hundreds of years."

Gregory and I smoked some the last of this ganja he was saving. It was awesome, a clear almost minty smell and lovely high with a spicy aroma to the bud and a clean brisk taste. It had a high that was almost preternatural.

"It's like a halo," he said. "Everything has like a halo around it."

"So this is the halo stone," I said. "It definitely shows forth the aura of radiance imbuing all things—which makes manifest—their true stellar origins."

Greg gave me a rather uncomfortable 'how am I supposed to react to that' look. "It is some of the nicest pot I have ever smoked," he said.

"A really clear intellectual high," I added, trying to regain credibility.

"You never get this kind of pot," Greg said. "This giant ganja has got to make it! It has got to rise to the challenge of standing up against the wind, to make stronger weed."

I enjoyed what I was learning from Gregory. Even through Gregory tried to hide it, his enthusiasm was contageious and so was his knowledge. Gregory not only knew the personal history of every plant but was always talking about the intelligence of the plants. He'd say things like: "Aren't these plants intelligent though. See how they have learned to put up shade leaves to protect their flowers from too much sun. That's because they evolved in a tropical climate."

"Man, it's hot enough around here for the plants to think they are in a tropical climate," I said.

"But I'm glad of that," Greg said "I think the heat makes them sweat out more THC. I read where someone said THC is like suntan lotion the plant manufactures to protect itself."

•••

To a certain extent, Greg believed in the lore of mistreating or stressing the plant to make it produce more THC.

"Maybe it's like mushrooms," I said. "Did you know that mushrooms exude psilocybin to keep flies from eating them."

Gregory raised his eyes in surprise.

"That's right." I continued, "Psilocybin, it turns out, is a kind of fly poison! It's a hallucinogen for human beings but poison for flies. Maybe, like they say, THC is exuded by pot as a response to stress."

"Is that what they say?" Greg asked with a note of incredulity in his voice. Gregory always had to think of himself as the only authority.

"Well I mean you yourself have said at times that you're supposed to stress the plants."

"Well I believe it to a certain extent," Greg said.

"What stress?" I asked.

"Well heat, for one thing, and just standing up in the wind. There are all kinds of other stuff I've heard of growers doing, like driving nails through the stocks. They say you should abuse them a little now and then, grab them and knock them around."

"Maybe it's like THC is a result of the plant exuding like endorphins to calm itself down," I said.

"Yeah, maybe it is." Greg agreed.

"They're like us," I said. "They self-medicate to reduce the unpleasant side effects due to stress in their lives."

"Yeah, that's a good theory." Greg agreed.

"Yeah maybe it's like endorphins for joggers." I said. "The plants sure were getting a lot of stress from the locusts eating on them, that's for damn sure."

At other times Greg would be out there with a ruler, measuring the distance between leaves on the plant or counting the number of blades per leaf.

"Check it out," he'd say. "This is the kind of plant intelligence that we are trying to breed for. See these Thais? They have long distances between the nodes, where the flowers will start growing from. This internodal distance is something the children learn from the parents."

He wanted plants with a long internodal distance so that they'd be easy to manicure.

•••

Besides the general population sprawl in the patch, there were the special hybrids which we put into the numerous hog and goat pens around the place. Some of these pens still had sheds and structures attached to them. To lift the roof off one of these and expose the rich unused dirt underneath, made the most excellent marijuana patch there is.

Gregory had one of his special prized Texas Twister Hybrid in a whole hog pen by itself. It was a big ungainly thing, already over eight feet tall. When the plant was about 3 feet tall, the stalk started bending over, and the limbs began to sag down like a willow tree. By the time the leafy boughs were heading toward the ground, Greg started tying them up. He did this in various ways. He tied wires to the pens or the wall, and let the limbs climb along the wires.

We had started referring to the giant sprawling ganga sending out

65

sinewy shoots sometimes as *The Creature in the Hog Pen*, or just the Creature, or the Creeping Viper.

Greg had trained four of the main side branches out and away from the central stock. He strung wire for them to be runners on. The branches were tied to the wires—what the French call *espalier*.

"God damn I hope this doesn't turn out to be another male," Gregory said. "The Texas Twister is a creeper, and it's one of my prize attempts to develop plants that are more like vines. You string these wires out and let them hang on the wires. That way they put more energy into extending their reach and getting really big, rather than putting their energy into building strong stock and branches to withstand the wind."

"I thought you said standing up against the wind makes for stronger pot." I said.

"Well, not in all cases. What's good for the ganja is not necessarily good for the creeper, har, har, har," he winked.

Another Texas twister he covered with a shell of chicken wire, and started the thin malleable limbs weaving and intertwining themselves up through the wire and let it crawl along that.

"This ought to be interesting," he said.

"When this starts to bloom, the buds will come straight up through the wires and just be sticking up out of the wire. We can harvest it by just clipping along, like sheering sheep."

•••

"You never did tell me where the stock for the Texas Twister Hybrid came from." I said one day.

"The Texas Twister hybrid was a true breeding creeper," Greg replied. "I came across this hybrid, quite by accident. It's a cross between a giant ganja and some other kind of weed from India I got

66

off a dealer. I don't know their origins. They looked a little like Thai seeds to me. But when I cross pollinated these two, I got the creeper."

•••

Before long we had pulled up enough premature male plants and hermaphrodites and dried them in the tackle shed, to get a couple of pounds of shake.

A couple of pounds! It felt so good to say that. A pound or an el-bee. God I liked the sound of that.

I loved the sound of the word 'Land' too. When I was telling friends about it, I called it the Land — loved saying it, the Land, — I'm going out to the *Land...* It was a word you said with a kind of reverence and closeness like you might say, 'my child',

The stuff we got was only early developing males and hermaph-rodites, and some kind of hash bush that Greg brought from his place in town that developed really quick. But God, I liked the sound of that even though it was only shake. I mixed in a little of Gregory's excellent home grown and it made a nice kind of working smoke. I gave Ruth a couple of ounces of this. That night she took the weed into town and easily sold it.

12

THE KATYDID CADENZA

Ruth was a good sculptor. She got books of all kinds of cicadas, grasshoppers and katydids. She did drawings; she studied the specimen. A couple of days later she brought back a little bamboo cage she bought at a flea market. She set it down on the picnic table under the tree on the back patio. It looked like a very small bird cage. It was built in the style of the elaborate Japanese architecture of a Zen temple. It had an onion-shaped roof gently curving upward. I carefully transferred a grasshopper from the Mason jar into the cage. The bamboo bars were thin as toothpicks, so you hardly noticed them as you looked through the spaces at the grasshopper. Ruth put a few leaves and some grass on the floor of the cage and a slice of cucumber for moisture.

Ruth and I sat out under the tree drinking lemonade and smoking some of the working mixture.

"According to this field guide here," Ruth said, proffering a heavy tome she had checked out of the library, "—*the Audubon Society Field Guide to North American Insects and Spiders*, what we're dealing with here is the short horned grasshopper."

"Damn those short horns anyway," I said.

"That's right. They're the ones that swarm," she said.

"But what's really gross, and I didn't know this about them, is that their color changes to get these dark spots on 'em because they eat so fast they can't digest all their food."

"Ooo gross," he said, squirming squeamishly.

"These bug books *are* kind of gross at first aren't they," she said.

"Yeah. Yeech. They are some kind of ugly alien beings."

"Yeah."

"All that armor."

"Yeah. They are like weird mechanical monsters," she said.

"But you know," I said, "if you look at them like robots...I took a class in robotics once and we looked at some of their mechanisms.

They've been around for a long time, and they have these incredible mechanisms. Their eyes, for example, the compound eyes are made up with thousands of lenses."

In a week, she brought back a sculpture about the size of a shoe box. It was shiny, made out of wire twisted and shaped into the frame of a grasshopper.

"I made this out of brass-alloy wire," she said.

"And look, —ta da," she said with a flourish of her hands like a maestro conducting an orchestra, "the head comes off, so you can open it up. It's really a cage!"

"God, that's marvelous," I said. The beautiful little frame model was a cage.

"I made it by taking the measurements out of the book," she said. "It's a ten times scale model. I used a pair of calipers and multiplied the measurements by ten to transfer them, pretty much exact, onto the wire frame."

"Wow."

"This is the chest" she said, pointing to the parts. "This is the abdomen, and these are the mandibles."

Rose looked pretty hip standing there in her free-box clothes, boots, and Smoky the Bear hat. She was really getting into explaining the parts like some kind of park ranger of the avant-garde.

"The middle section is the thorax, from which, like all insects, they have six legs and two sets of wings," she continued, looking like some school girl making a science presentation. "I've got just the outline, of the wings folded down—shaped in wire—here. You see? And the angle of the big hind legs is at that most cocked-up point, right before they are about to jump."

"God, it looks great. Beautiful." I said. "Reminds me of that big wrought-iron grasshopper they have in Chapultapec park in Mexico City."

"Exactly!" she said, excitedly. "I was inspired by that one. I saw it down there last year, in fact, when I drove the Bronco down, on the trip to import fabric for the dress shop. I liked it so much, I sent a postcard of it to myself."

We transferred a short-horned male grasshopper from the bamboo cage into the wire-frame icon.

It seemed to like its new home. The critter let out an intense, loud, sustained, hard-edged white noise blast that seemed to lasted fully 10 seconds.

"Wow, listen to its sound." I said. "Grasshopper is loud!"

"Yeah! God damn, that's intense!" she said.

"It looks like the ghost in the machine," I said.

"Or the mechanical bird in the gilded cage," she said.

"It looks damn good to me." I said. "I'm ready to start praying to the idol. I'm ready to put false gods before my lord in vain!"

13

The Background Hisss of Summer

Ruth often brought a bag of peyote buttons out with her. It was cool to eat peyote out at the farm because you felt safe, isolated —

wasn't anybody going to be coming up that road. The gate was locked, they'd need the combination. You could get totally whacked out of your skull.

I'd start feeling nervous when she placed the dried-up gnarly-looking cactus apples on the table. I remembered the horrendous taste, and how you always have to barf your guts out before you see God. Another thing is, I didn't usually like to trip with anybody. You have to really trust the person you're gonna trip with, and I trusted nobody. Least of all lovers. Also I am a day tripper, I didn't like to trip at night. So, though I was intimidated, I was thankful, at least, that we would be tripping during the day. I ate a little, enough to be sociable, enough to get high but not enough to, go over the edge.

We smoked a little tea to take the nauseating alkaline taste out of our mouths and to tide us over until the hallucinogen came on. Ruth did a ritual, wafting burning cedar incense into the four corners. The marijuana smoke mixed with the cedar incense and floated up into the still air. We started to make some conversation to bridge the silence.

"Have you noticed," Ruth began, "that there is a big difference between the sounds of the grasshoppers and the cicadas at night and during the day. During the day they are really loud."

"That's for damn sure," I said. " People who grow up around this all their lives, it must either drive them nuts or it must do something to their minds, get their minds aligned or something."

"I think," she said, "they rub, as they sit there. They rub their legs together..."

"Yeah that's the uh, stridulating," I interjected. "It's called stridulating, I read it in the book you got."

"Yeah," she offered, tenuously agreeing.

"And they rub that big hairy legs across their wings," I continued. We listen in to the caterwauling of all the katydids. "It's like a bowed instrument."

"Ahh," she said.

"And the reason why the crickets and cicada sounds are different during the day and at night," I told her, "is because they are tied to the temperature. I read in the book the other day you can compute the actual temperature from the sounds they make. If you count the number of chirps in 14 seconds and you add 42 to it, you get the actual temperature."

"I don't believe you," she teased. "You're making that up."

"No, that's what it says."

We listened to the staccato caterwauling of the cicadas and the crickets all a jumble in the hisss of the summer's day.

"I don't know how they count it though," I said.

We both were listening intently. Cicada was loud. The sound was endless, and it wavered and shifted as if there were varying pockets of density in space. At times it seems like the insects were making a concerted effort to fracture a wall or pierce some kind of veil with their endless sound beams.

"How do you count chirps in that?" I asked. "You must have to have an oscilloscope of something."

She looked thoughtful for a moment. "Do you have a watch with a second hand?"

"No, I don't *even* have a watch. But I can count seconds."

"All right let's give it a try," she said

"O.K."

"Number of chirps in 14 seconds," she said.

"OK. Ready. Set. Go." I said.

There didn't seem to be any break or discrete bursts in the wall of sound washing over us.

"Oh it's impossible," Ruth said. "My god."

"How do they come up with that. I wonder," I said.

"Do you think they could like slow it down or something? Oh, my god!?" she said.

"They must have to record it and play it back," I said.

"Or maybe if you just start like on a cold day," she said.

"Or maybe," I said, "they just mean the whole burst. It's 14 *bursts* of chirps, like these are really long because these are day crickets. Or maybe at night they are not so close together and shorter."

"All right I'm gonna give it another try," she said. "Tell me when it's time."

"All right I'll start counting 1001, 1002, 1003, ...That's 14 seconds. How many chirps?"

"The way I figured it out if I can just go like this," she said and she raised her hand and brought it down like a maestro giving the down stroke, "It's like there's 5 chirps every time I go like that."

"Oh, yeah. Estimate. Good." I said.

So as I was counting, she was raising and lowering her hand abruptly. "I don't know. I think I got 45. So what would that be?" She asked.

"Well then 45 and 42 would make it about 87 degrees," I said. "It's about right."

"Let's go over to the porch. Lets look at the thermometer."

She walked up onto the back porch and read it of.

"89 degrees! Not bad."

"Yeah pretty close."

"Damn, they've really got it down to a science don't they." she said kind of disappointed, with a kind of sadness for something that had just been quantified out of mystery.

With scientific certitude I concluded: "Yep. The sound that the crickets and the cicadas make *is* directly related to the temperature."

"Yeah" said, "Mr. Know-it-All, the hotter it gets the louder they get."

"Yeah but now with the Cicada," I mused, not taking up the tease, "you don't have discrete chirps that you can count. Here we have continuous white noise trilling. We'd have to do some kind of harmonic analysis to find the mean frequency."

Ruth gave me that kind of glazed-over bewildered stare I had seen often enough in my life. Oh, oh, I am slipping into science again. I was starting to feel nauseated and rushy.

"It would be like trying to find the mean frequency of the back ground hiss of summer." I mumbled. The itchy restlessness was setting in — upsetting body sensations were running up and down the back of my neck.

"Listen Ruth, I'm gonna take a little walk-about and check on the patch. I'll be back in a little while." I had never invited Ruth to the patch. I wanted to make sure she was innocent of all that —in case they captured and tortured her. Besides my partner had forbade it.

I arose creakily and headed back into the animal pens. I worried about leaving her all by her lonesome, but she was used to it. I'm sure my eyes looked wild. One eye looks out and the other looks in. There was just so much to explore rather than give your attention to one person.

There was some kind of struggle between Ruth and me. A friendly but gut-wrenching battle of archetypes, the mother and the father, the lovers. God I hope she didn't want to have sex, that was the last thing on my mind. When I have psychedelics I can't perform to save my soul. On psychedelics I became a philosopher and a mystic and was like as not to cogitate in public (cogitate cogitate, throw up all the food you ate.) I could sense a hollowness within, a tunnel opening up. My first priority was not whether but where I was going to barf. I didn't need anyone to hold my head.

"The background hiss of summer, the background hiss of summer," I kept thinking, against the complex texture of bright summer grasses, shot through with bursts and buzzes of white noise shaped by crickets and cicadas. I did the snake shuffle, boots dragging along the ground sending out plenty of snake warning vibrations and crackling through dried reeds.

I had become acclimatized to the country. I wore loose white cotton and a big wide brimmed Panama hat made of loose weave straw. I had more of a body awareness. If a tick or any insect got on me, I could immediately sense it and gracefully, absent-mindedly remove the critter. Being always alert for snakes, led to a kind of enhanced awareness of the environment. This simplified life of hauling water and tending plants, and the intense heat seemed to slow time down somehow. I had become increasingly alert to the marijuana world, the kind of alertness, as they say in the *Tao Te Ching*, that is necessary to the mastery of a subject.

God damn! It is hot. Every day in the high nineties and low 100s. There was a terrible drought in Texas and we really had to stay on top of the watering. At least until hurricane season.

The background hiss of summer.

Yes

The background hiss of summer rises with heat.

If you listen in to it, into the cicadas, what you get are these layers of silence and sound that seem to travel. Walls of noise that are thrown up, then vanish with an abruptness that is so sudden that your mind keeps on going like a vector into silence. It's like when you look out onto the road and see the heat rising in wavering undulating columns. Like a mirage, the heat makes the landscape shift and move through a lens of air. You could actually feel the shifting of the microclimate, the movement of the heat. But now the mirage of heat was actually being translated by the cicadas into a wavering and shifting in the wall of sound, in the cosmic buzz moving through all things. It was like the cosmic buzz, —the heat permeating the universe, left over from the explosion of the big bang — was a fundamental and all the things that lived up and down the order of heat niches were harmonics of this background heat buzz. A kind of biological *aufbau*, orbital filling. The ever widening circles of matter circulating around smaller circles, quarks around energy, electrons around neutrons, molecules around atoms, cells around molecules, organs around cells, beings around organs, families around beings, communities around families, ever expanding outward chains of being like a pebble dropped into pond.

Are the cicadas attuned to the cosmic buzz? I asked myself. What do they know of the cosmic buzz?! It's as if the insects and plants are saying, "I've got a secret."

So I began to do drugs and wander the fields and take dictation from the background hiss of summer. —pretty crazy out there, many is the time I would imagine my own obituary, walking around out there. One of them went like this.

Snake-Bitten Philosopher Dies
The white clad body of philosopher Walker
Underwood was found in a field outside Manor. He was
on a walk with his dog, when bitten by a rattlesnake. The
wool-gathering graduate student of the University of
Texas, who many said had been struck by god, was
thought to have been distracted and not heeding the
snake's hissing warning signs.
Underwood is remembered as a regular in the Student
Union and other places on campus for holding forth in
spontaneous public address.

"I remembered thinking what a lost soul he was," said friend
Jules Windish. "He was the fool on the hill. He always wore white to
identify with the working class peon. I had to admire his ideas and
for trying to turn the university into a Platonic agora in which men
openly and earnestly discussed philosophy and religion."

I have pulled together some of the experiences in a long poem-
like entity called Hyperspectral/the Dirac Satori.

I had a lot of time on my hands that summer and I started
exploring concrete poetry on the typewriter.

I also got these ideas about trying to write about the Satori.
Seemed like that was a worthwhile subject. The satori I experienced
while on peyote and other psychedelics, and sometimes while not on
drugs. Satori is a philosophical moment, in which you feel your
presence in the universe.

The poem would start out with the narrator, the I wanting to
understand the archetypes of perception that I was seeing in the
psychedelic.

I started off with some kind of philosophical quest, to know
something of the transcendental reality we all have a right to know at
the basis behind the chatter, I started off with the desire of a physics

student at that time, — the first generation to grow up with a readily excepted view of relativity, and quantum mechanics, and hyper-spaces — but mainly I began to want to write a poem that was about perception and about the idea of word as object, like the way that we see through a narrator's view as a kind of word as programming the human computer to see. And of course that lead to notation.

Word as object is notation. But even more than that I wanted to have a poem that gave a world view of someone that was slowed down and walking through the forest and starting to see the web of life, or the semiotics of symbiosis.

So I conceived of a poem which had a narrator, but the narrator maybe shifted to Gaia being the narrator, or the narrator emphasizing with Gaia. But it was something that was much bigger than Gaia, I called it Noo-sphere first spoken about in Tieard de Chardin. But that hasn't been updated and it came to me that a structure might be the Green Bank, well it would be a kind of seed bank and it was in the parameters of the Green Bank formula that I got a picture of this hyperspectral aspect of communication to the physical spectral. I also wanted to find a more ancient basis for it in the Vedas, which is to say in the origin of grammar as a way of structuring reality.

I'd sit there at my typewriter and take dictation from the waves of cicada rising and falling and I wrote this narrative poem. *

And in writing that poem I came to know their secret! The song of the grasshoppers is a harmonic of the white noise left over by the big bang!

"That's the secret of the Grasshopper's trilling!" I shouted aloud to nobody in particular.

* I have pulled the poems and narrative together in a 2nd book titled: The Secret of the Cicadas' Song. -- WU

78

The background hiss of summer, is crickets and grasshoppers stridulating, looking for the resonance frequency of summer, so that they can drive it, to create a message that gets transmitted through the leftover ubiquitous background heat radiation of the universe and travel quickly to other planets."

Yes. That's it.

Do you think there can be any truth to that?

I've got to tell somebody, anybody, her. Got to tell Ruth.

Yeah Rrrright. I could see myself telling her.

14

CLOSE ENCOUNTERS OF THE THIRD KIND

Somehow I got back to the house after walking around in the fields and patch. I remembered being delighted at a Japanese lantern Ruth had put over the bare bulb in the patio tree. Uh, oh, home improvements. Once that starts who knows where it will end. Ruth had even made some lemonade.

Round about dusk, the cicadas were really wailing and so was the little unit in the katydid cage.

"You know what I'm gonna do," I said to Ruth.

"No what."

"I'm gonna record the cicada sound and play it back out into the patch.

"I'm gonna stick a microphone into the cage with our pet grass-hopper here and I'm going to record it on tape. And then I'm going to play it back through an amplifier. I'll blast it back into the patch to see if that will scare the locusts off. Maybe the other grasshoppers will think that it is some giant Godzilla grasshopper come into their midst."

"I wonder if anyone has ever tried that before," she asked.

"I don't know. Seems if their sound has any meaning at all, if you made it louder, they must associate it with bigness."

I caught a ride back into town with Ruth and the Bugle. I would return with Gregory. I bought a small microphone at Radio Shack. When I met Gregory at Lenora's, I told him about this idea to use sound to scare off the locusts.

At first, Greg looked at me as if I were insane.

"Well it's all I can think of," I said defensively. "We've tried just about everything else."

"Well maybe," Greg conceded. "Come to think of it, I once read in the Bible where they used trumpets to bring down the walls of Jerico."

"And there are stories of monks in Tibet who can focus sound energy." I added.

"And anyway we got to start thinking about pot rustlers," Greg said. "Might be a doggone good way to get rid of them too. Put speakers out into the patch and crank the sucker up."

Greg borrowed his mother's really good tape recorder with Dolby, to record it with that. I was surprised that Greg didn't think it was a dumb idea. I thought, maybe Greg is coming under the spell of the background hisss of summer too. It melts down people's minds.

It was a right of passage for me too, to find myself at Lenora's and to feel a sense of relief being there on my own terms, to finally be operating out of my own place. Lenora would never have said anything, but I felt when I had been crashing occasionally at her place that I was right on the edge of overstaying my welcome. I was proud I got my own place. I was glad to be out of her hair. Not that she'd ever say anything.

I wanted to hear the latest installment in the story about the guy with the famous Stradivarius cello.

Lenora had her aging eccentric father living out the last days of his life in her home. The man had been a world famous musician and had taught at Radcliff. Lenora set him up in a bedroom with an attached bathroom in the front of the house. Her house was densely filled with musical instruments and paraphernalia. Everywhere there was sheet music stacked neatly on open shelves. She had two huge baby grand pianos and a spinet piano. There were heavy tapestries on the wall. Lenora had surrounded herself with a salon to rival Sarah Bernhardt.

In his room the old man had a photographic portrait of Einstein. In the picture the great wild-haired scientist is wearing a cool leather jacket with a high collar. Back in those days, the old Russian college music professor had let the great German physicist sit in, with his violin, sometimes, in their quartet. (The old musicologist had pronounced that: "Einstein was pretty good for an amateur.")

But by now, the always-eccentric old father was becoming senile. It was not uncommon on any visit over there to see the old music professor trying to give cello lessons to the dog. Lenora's dog is a huge great Dane called Big Dog. Big Dog was not an apt pupil, though occasionally Big Dog would hold still for a serenade, and at times would even moan and whine to join in and it was a duet: Cello with Dog. This would have been funny except I knew it was driving

Lenora nuts. It was a lesson that all of Lenora's friends were getting about old age, and responsibility. The way Lenora bore up under it, was a lesson in grace. I performed various services around the house, in order to ensure I did not appear, even remotely, to be an added burden, but was helping out.

The old man had these two old rare Stradivarius Cellos that he had been given by various admiring royalty and patrons in the old country. It was that summer that the old guy had to be put in an intensive care home, and Lenora had to sell one of the cellos. She sent it to Sotheby's in New York to be auctioned because the cost of the insurance was getting out of hand.

Lenora in her great generosity and sponsorship for all music, had given it to a friend of hers who was a second string musician touring in a New York Summer Philharmonic orchestra to take it to Sotheby's saying he could use it on the tour until he got back to New York. I had gone to the concert in Austin, and when the second fiddle began to play this amazing axe, it shocked everybody in the orchestra and audience with its pristine clear sound.

For weeks after that, the musician would call Lenora every night extolling the virtues of the Strad cello as a musical instrument. Night after night he called singing the praises of and going on and on about how much he loved the Stradivarius cello and how much he loved the sound, going into exquisite detail talking about the lacquer on the wood, and the purity of the sound that everybody noticed the first time he struck a note on it, and how it was just the finest instrument he had ever had the honor of playing and how much he hated to give it up. But of course he couldn't afford it. It was appraised at a quarter of a million, and eventually the little cello player went rogue, and wouldn't give it up, and he had to be interdicted on tour and the instrument taken away from him.

Gregory and I drove back out to the land. We brought out an old stereo amplifier Gregory had. He also brought a pair of walkie-talkies he had picked up at an army surplus sale — Greg had driven down to a big sale at Kelly Air Force base in San Antonio.

We also unloaded two big, wood-cabinet loudspeakers his mother wasn't using. We toted one big speaker way out to the patch. Unfurling a long strand of speaker wire from a spool, we attached the speaker back to the amplifier, which was plugged into the house socket.

The mischievous grin on Gregory's face told me that Greg really liked the synergy of using sound in both the insect and pot rustler maintenance program.

"Go on back to the house," Greg said, "and turn it up. I'll tell you what it sounds like over these walkie-talkies."

We cranked it up. The amplified cicada sound was horrendous. It was a loud, stinging, nerve-wracking, grilling of hard edged white noise, full of nothing but the nasty odd harmonics. Greg and I both half believed that if they cranked that sucker up, the loud grasshopper trilling would make the locust think that indeed a giant grasshopper had come into their midst. Presumably the locusts eating the patch would all get scared of the giant and run away. Addled brain drug-science — of course it didn't work.

Gregory and I fell into a panic a few days later, after a couple more of plants got wiped out. We started a whole second wave of plants in cans, thinking we might loose everything and have to start over to salvage the season. We put the cans out in the starter beds under shade cloth so the grasshoppers couldn't get to them. The locusts continued knocking off branches left and right in the main population.

Another thing that worried us was, we were starting to use a lot of water. The underground reservoir out back by the patch was as big as a swimming pool. Even so, I pulled an average of 200 — 5 gallon buckets a day out of it, and its level was getting low.

As I pulled up more and more buckets, I got stronger and stronger. I got this marvelous long stroke going, reaching way up high on the chain and pulling it, eerily creaking over the pulley.

I began to get right feral. Maybe feral is not the right word — I wasn't going around foaming at the mouth, or biting the heads off of chickens and sucking their blood or anything. I was just feeling wild with so much energy. I was feeling well balanced and alive and my awareness was up. It was like being a criminal in the service of nature (and in the service of myself) and this nature-wise / street-wise awareness was a feeling so unnatural that it felt almost feral.

It was so hot that I would work in a little pair of shorts. I started to get tanned. When the cistern ran dry Greg had me climb down into it and scrub the walls and repair it. Then we had a load of drinking water put in there as well as filling up the galvanized tank. Greg and I had a lot of discussion about the water man coming onto the land in his truck. We decided to drive into Austin to check out the Travis County Water Resources Management Bureau. The facility turned out to be just a big depot with a lot of trucks in it. The facility was part county and part Texas Highway department. It was their business to deliver water to country people who didn't have their own wells. Perfectly ordinary.

I was out there when the man came in the tank truck with the load of water. I met him and signed the receipt.

I enjoyed using this good clean cold water I pulled up from the underground in the cistern to water my house garden. I would go out in the garden, take all my clothes off and by throwing handfuls of water up in the air, make it rain! I began to garden in nothing at all, throwing double handfuls of water high into the sky and to watch it spangle down all over me in the sunshine. It got me clean, and watered the garden and cooled me off all at the same time.

One Sunday morning on the front porch I started communicating with a mocking bird. I could tell it was a mocking bird because it started mimicking the sounds of another bird near by. Only it wasn't quite right on. I decided I would get into the act and started to whistle the theme from Close Encounters of the 3rd Kind, which was very popular then.

da ^{daa} $_{duh}$ da $_{duh}$ ^{dah}

And pretty soon the mocking bird had picked up the whole phrase and whistled it back.

I felt like I could talk to the animals.

15

BIG G

The next time Ruth was out, I said to her "This whole episode building the Grasshopper amuses the hell out of me."

"Thanks." she said. "We tried."

"Your little wire-frame sculpture was a nice piece of work. You did a good job."

"It was a lark." she said.

"What we are really trying to do is build a protector or guardian for the patch," I said, "and what I'm thinking, is, maybe it wasn't a big enough offering."

I stuck my face down into hers and said, "What if we made a bigger one."

Her eyes widened with the concept, "Build a bigger one?"

"Yeah. Build one as big as a table," I said, "or ...or as big as...as a Volkswagen Beetle!" I checked her out to see if she was interested. "We've got a lot of old car parts and stuff out here. We've got the whole cultch."

"The cultch?" she asked. "What's that?"

"That's the cultural mulch." I said

I made a gesture with my hands suggesting a processes of big, hard-edged, metal junk objects gradually subsiding down into dust. "You know, it's that accumulation of old mechanical junk and tractor parts and furniture that you have around any farm. When you pile it all in one place, that's what people call, the cultch. There's a bunch of it over there where Gregory dragged it over and used it as part of the fence line. And there's a big gully full of it, out-back of the barn. We're talking antique, post Industrial Revolution junk here!"

"Yeah, I've looked through that stuff, up by the fence," she said. "You've got some neat junk!"

"Well, what about it," I said.

I looked at her with enthusiasm in my eyes. She's probably doing this just to please me. I liked her too, and it was nice to have the company. I find it difficult showing love, so I made it look like a money deal. It would not cost me all that much. The lids I made up for her would be only a mixture of shake with a little of Gregory's finest thrown in. Gregory had given me a couple of ounces to try. It turned out to be a very popular working smoke.

"Build a LARGE icon," I said, "of the Grasshopper out of wire, chicken fence, car parts and wood? I could give you a few pounds."

"For a few pounds? You bet!" she said excitedly.

"Onward through the fog!" I said.

"To the cultch!" she said.

Over the weeks we dragged out quite a morass of wire, chicken fence, car parts and wood. Soon there was quite a lot of stuff back there, leaning on the walls of the house and festooned around the patio and she was becoming more and more enthusiastic about it.

"What's all this shit," Gregory said one day. He was getting tired of seeing the reconstituted cultch around the patio.

"Ruth is building a really BIG grasshopper sculpture." I said.

"Oh, Christ."

• • •

Ruth started coming out to the place even more often. She started collecting more, and looking long at things. Staring at them while her mind fit them into the sculpture of the giant cicada, which we had started calling Big-G. She got more car parts at her favorite junk yards and from her greaser pals. She got headlights for eyes, and she began to accumulate grills again, adding to her already extensive collection. She thought these would be good for the fluted body parts.

The project took a turn of epic proportions when two workmen, driving a dump truck load of construction site debris to the county dump up the road, decided to save themselves the rest of the drive and pocket the $50 dump fee. They drove past the unlocked gate of the farm, drove half way up to the house on the driveway and just dropped the load on the land

There, lying atop the pile of construction site debris, was a beat up playground slide at least 12 feet tall. They must have been taking apart an old school yard. I knew immediately it would look good in the sculpture as the Grasshopper's hind leg!

I hitchhiked into town to get Ruth to come out and see it. I would need her help to get the slide up to the house before Gregory saw it.

When Ruth saw it she totally got it, too.

"Look at how the slide slopes up then comes down almost straight where the ladder is," I said.

"Yeah."

"That would make a perfect leg for the giant grasshopper!"

"Wow! I see what you mean."

• • •

"Man, that means it's gonna be really big," she said after we got the slide back up to the house. "We're talking major work here."

"Well, here, I got a LB for you to get started."

I gave her a pound then and there to seal the deal. She stashed it behind the spare in the trunk of her car. Since she knew all kinds of people she turned that lb in one night.

• • •

Gregory was really pissed when he saw the mess that the construction workers had left. He started cussing about the lack of security around here. "You don't seem to understand man, we could get busted. Anybody snooping around could turn us in for a reward."

I showed him a box with the address of the construction company on it. Gregory got into his car, to go into town and cuss them out on the phone and tell them to haul it away.

I said, "Get the construction company to pay *us* to haul it away. That way, they wouldn't have to deal with it, we wouldn't have to have them come out here again."

The construction company foreman insisted on sending out his boys to clean up the mess that they had created on the land. Nobody mentioned the slide.

The next day Ruth was back with a portable acetylene welder that she got from one of her mechanic friends and set it up by the patio under the tree and started welding pieces together. She was wearing dark goggles, boots, heavy jean shirt and large Mule Skin welding gloves up to her elbows.

I got a hose and ran it around from the drinking tank in case she started a fire. She cut the fender of an old gutted rusted car body loose. More and more car parts fell under her torch, that summer. She worked on Big G for most of June and part of July. It is a slow time in growing. The plants are juvenile don't even differentiate sex. Nothing to do but wait and hope the locusts don't eat them.

She welded on the six little scuttling legs made of bent and rusted re-bar. I helped her use a rented pipe bender. At first it just looked like a sinister barbecue pit sitting on wrought iron legs.

The playground slide she cut in two down the middle to make the sweeping hind legs of the grasshopper. These she welded onto each side of a long truss made of pipe which was the main grasshopper body. With the slide put in place for the hind legs it started to look like the skeleton structure of some kind of demented helicopter-insect.

The gay bikers gave her big swatches of cowhide leather, which she ended up saturating with a kind of lacquer so it was shiny and crinkly and had a flaky, scaly, peeling, skin-like, quality to it. In some places she attached it taunt and in other places she draped it in loose folds over the metal tubing truss.

• • •

Spectral Reflectance

Ruth kept working on Big-G.

"This is the most challenging project I've ever worked on," she said.

"Yeah. You're doing great."

Next thing was the eyes, these many faceted bubble eyes. She brought out boxes of colored glass. She started making the compound eyes, the 2,000-and-something lens compound eyes.

"Look at this picture," she said. The grasshoppers have mosaic eyes, not continuous like ours. They see things in a mosaic with these big eyes."

"I wonder if they have a problem with vapor trails." I said.

"You know what I'm gonna do for the eye?" she said.

"No, what."

Ruth touched this large spherical piece of white mesh. It looked like a colander with a slightly bigger weave. "I've got this mesh" she said. "It bends pretty good. I'm gonna shape it more spherical, and glue bits of colored glass into the holes."

"Wow, that's a lot of work," I said. "Are you sure you really want to do that much. I'd settle for something easier."

"No I don't mind," she said. "It's part of the job. It's got to get better and better. It will give these eyes the effect of spectral reflectance."

"Oooo. Specular reflectance. What you said."

She looked proud of herself, teasing me with a big word. "Yep gotta have specular reflectance," she said. "That's what really makes them look like bug eyes. And it will too, I've never gotten this many bits of colored glass this close together before."

"Wow, man, you're really going for the detail."

"Well, it's no big deal," she said. "It's not brain surgery. It's not like I was having to create a real grasshopper *robot*, although this would be a good start for such a robot. It would be cool if it had pneumatic legs and could walk around, and it had circuitry—one that could, you know, have video cameras behind its eyes. On this one the eyes will be big enough to get inside and see out of."

"Wow I'd like to see that."

"Me too."

"Don't get sick sniffing all that glue."

Ruth thought for a moment. "You know I could get somebody to help me if I had a little money to pay them. Rose would probably help. Maybe I ought to bring Rose out here."

"Yeah. Sure," I said. "What do you need?"

"Couple more ounces of some weed."

"You got it."

"Before it gets too big, to move, Ruth said, "I want to orient this critter to get the best light on the eyes."

"Well if we're gonna keep it back here on the patio, we could face it this way, so it gets direct morning sunlight from over there."

Big G extended from the porch clear out to the side of the house, as long as the room. It looked like it was leaning on the house, looking around it toward the eastern sun. We could pull ourselves up the slide steps, and step out onto the porch roof. From there we could scramble up onto the roof of the house and lay up there, arms draped over the peak of the roof with field glasses like outlaws keeping a watch over the hideout.

• • •

Gregory thought it was the weirdest thing. And he was pissed that somebody came out to the farm. But I told Greg, straight out and true, that they didn't know where the patch was.

And Ruth was not to be denied. She was in a passion, she was working on the project of her life.

• • •

Rose and her boyfriend! came out. They set themselves up in the big room. They got a lot of work done on the eyes. It was like a nice male and female quilting B, to which the men had been invited.

Then Rose and her boyfriend were up most of the night getting into hot and heavy sex. Rose yelled out in orgasm several times in the night. You could hear Rose moaning in the next room "O, OH, GOD DAMMMN."

It was embarrassing. She moaned with the abject perfidiousness of the damned, of a lost soul abandoned to the experienced hands of a torturer. She must have known we could hear her and couldn't care less. THUMP, THUMP, THUMP "O, AH OH, AH , O MY GaaAWWWd." It sounded like he was banging her head against the wall. Then Rose started hyperventilating and moaning at the same time.

I found it interesting. It made me think about how far from being super-satisfying my "relationship" was with Ruth.

I noticed that Ruth seemed to be getting turned on by it too. Perhaps there was some kind of competition between the two women to see who could be the loudest, because Ruth started carrying on, too, when she and I started getting into sex. "O hah uh hah! O Jesus honey, oh my gawd!" I was kind of proud of that.

92

Radio Dude Ranch of the Air

The next morning we were all feeling good, a couple of couples feeling close, sitting around the patio eating a little breakfast. After a while, under the direction of Ruth, we started up working again on Big-G's eyes. As the day progressed, the usual chorus of cicadas, grasshoppers and crickets put up a wall of sound in the background. We all ate some peyote and while waiting for it to come on, shared a joint. I started thinking about a Radio Ranch. The heat was already intense and the cicada sound was exceedingly intense.

"Man that's intense," someone said.

I was trying to make some conversation and at the same time tease Ruth a bit, so I said: "This sculpture is going to be as famous as Watts Tower. Me and Ruth are going to open a dude ranch with rides."

Ruth gave me a look that said, what is this boy up to.

"No, I'm serious. We have got to come up with some kind of legal, and what they call an ecologically-sustainable, steady-state income source.

I looked around to see if they liked that.

"Me and Ruth are going to start a kind of radio dude ranch of the air, a kind of radio farm. Instead of raising plants or livestock we farm radio, we record the natural radio sounds of the earth and the sounds of the wind on plants and animals all around us and transmit it back to the cities."

"Huh," she said. "First I've heard of this."

Rose started joining in on teasing Ruth too.

"I could see it." Rose said. "A camp for teenagers that offered the rural farm experience for young people.

Bless her she really wants to see me and Ruth together.

"Hiking," her boyfriend put in.

"Horseback riding," Rose ventured.

"Swimming," Ruth added.

"Back packing, overnights, lose weight, get fit," Rose added.

We were all starting to feel the effects coming on.

"What will we call it?" Ruth asked, playing along.

"Camp Kinakookie," Rose's boyfriend said with disdain.

"No I got a better name," Ruth said, pausing for effect, "we could call it Camp Katydid."

"Camp Katydid, ooh, I like that," I said. "Yeah, but instead of raising livestock or vegetation or even entertaining dudes we'd collect sounds."

I started thinking about the money I'd be making when all the pot came in. I COULD start my own radio station. In my mind's eye I saw the wooden structure of the old windmill out back transforming itself into a tall steel radio tower.

"Here's what the people would do at the Radio Dude Ranch. We'd have them sitting on the porch fishing for sounds.

"See, my idea is that heat...HEAT, (said in a loving and respectful way like a gentle old thermodynamacist might say it) heat moving among the insects, is a conductor. It causes them to change their sound."

I leaned forward and held my hand in the air as if it were the bag of a balloon.

"Here's how it would work. We'd get some of those helium balloons filled with gas and hang a radio transmitter microphone from its underside. The weight of the little radio transmitter just compensating for the lift of the balloon. We would have it be so well balanced and sensitive that it could chase the bubbling thermals along and it would radio back the sounds of the cicadas and the crickets to us. We could see the balloon moving through the fields and reel it back in or move it around on some invisible fish line."

Walker's eyes brightened. "A big part of the experience would be 3D sound, and in order to really capture this 3D effect of the symphony, you have to be right out in it."

"As the balloon moved along, drifting silently through the landscape, it would pick up the various distinct sound activity of the insects and birds and frogs and winds in the trees. And we'd make tapes and sell them to radio! That'd be far out, wouldn't it?"

They all looked at I like I was crazy.

"People who lived in the city might really like to have the sounds of a summer night broadcast to their radios in stereo 3D or even quadraphonic. Maybe a lot of them miss it. Certainly it is something that really sets life in the country apart."

"Yeah, that would be really far out, man," said Rose's boyfriend.

Ruth said, "Yeah, it would be really neat if we could put a little camera on it and let that float along and tape pictures of the hollows and what not that the sensor balloon floated through."

"We could be like cubists with multi-faceted eyes and see thermals with our ears!" I said.

"Dig it!" shouted Ruth, who liked the cubists.

"What's that again?" asked Rose. "Say it again."

"Cubists with multi-faceted eyes can see thermals with their ears!"

"Whooooo."

"Haaa haa."

"You know, but really folks," I said, "it's more spiritual than that.

I want to see the shape of heat that conducts the sound. The sounds are vibrating and shifting themselves. If you could picture the sound as just a shape of energy in space, you would say that the shape tapered off evenly around its edges with distance, blending with the environment."

I thought about the black body problem, how it modeled heat as little spring oscillators in the surface walls.

"These changes in the sound wall are a flood of sound, being generated by all the little cicadas standing still and playing inside the big thermal shape." I said.

It really did seem true to me. It really did seem like we could see with our ears this kind of cloud or symphony hall that was filled with thousands of tiny chanters all trying to harmonize with each other. At least see with metaphor, it was just the black body problem writ large.

I was starting to slip into a theatrical mode. Sometimes, on peyote, instead of getting super-introspective I go outside myself and become what for me feels like being hyper-extroverted. I go mega, my ego sets in, and I will start performing. What is coming over me? I saw I had a captive audience. We are feeling close and loose and it's time to style out. Time to bring off something revolutionary. What if I did take the money I made from growing and selling marijuana and started a natural radio station.

"We'd start raising Natural Radio." I said. "By Natural Radio, I mean basically this Very Low Frequency stuff I have been recording along with the natural sounds."

"What would you call it," Ruth asked. I couldn't tell whether she was just being supportive or if she really was interested.

"K-slow. KSLO" I said.

I waved my hand, palm facing my face as if dragging a banner across the sky behind an airplane with slogan on it: "The natural radio that slows time down." I could see they were having trouble with this so I hit them with another: "Anti-frenetic alternative music for your listening pleasure."

"We'd be doing something good for the whole planet," I said. I drew myself up into a straight backed revolutionary pose. "We'd be able to subvert and overthrow the tyranny of clock-based city-time and present people with circadian rhythms that are more natural. It would be revolutionary."

"Nhya Ha ha," I said wringing my hands like a matinee villain, and then making dragging one leg along like the slimeball dope pusher Aqualung in a conspiracy I said, "It would be insect music to fry your brain!"

My mind started racing ahead, imagining a giant radio tower going higher and higher above the windmill, spending the money from growing pot to start up a radio station. Perhaps I could get an associate from my days in the small press, Lorenzo Milam to sponsor us to get our own license. Maybe he would consider it a good thing to put his money into. I could see myself doing a pitch to Lorenzo, him looking on suspicious but amazed under his curly hair probably white by now, sitting in his wheel chair. "The idea is that we would make tapes of spherics which are a kind of natural radio, and make tapes of natural sounds, cicadas, frogs, birds, just what was going on in real nature and broadcast these sounds to the world or syndicate these sounds to the radio networks of the world." I started using this opportunity of talking to my friends to practice my pitch to Lorenzo.

"It would be revolutionary. It would perhaps help the old people who remembered the country. It would remind them of those times and it would slow things down out there."

Peyoteros' Obligato

I felt the peyote coming on. I started to pace a little around the patio. I felt uncomfortable addressing these people. O god, I'm going to cogitate in public, I thought. I started to think of things from very far away, an almost evolutionary perspective.

Rose, true to her ever-contrary nature, interjected, "But you know Radio is a kind of pollution, too."

I was thinking about eyes and the evolution of the eye. "You know," I said, "I used to worry about getting hit by all these rays, all this radio and satellite communication going on all over the earth. But when I looked it up they found that the absorption spectra of electromagnetic spectrum either was reflected off water or passed through it like it wasn't even there. But there was a huge dip in the absorption curve right in the optical part of the spectrum. This provided a *window* in which the eye evolved so that it could pick up an enormous amount of resolution while at the same time being a very small detector."

I stood up and started prancing around. I took the stage. I made an elaborate expansive gesture to the sky.

"I'd like to hijack a grasshopper," I said, "and take it joy riding through the summer hiss."

The three old friends, Ruth, Rose and her boyfriend, were sitting around the table. Rose and her boyfriend looked at each other, then both turned to look at Ruth.

"I'd like to ride a grasshopper," I said, "take it out in the morning, keep it out all day."

They all turned their head in unison to look at me.

I could see that they were giving me weird looks like I had just made some horrible social gaff. Better not let them see me do that, I thought. I'll travel up inside my head, and try to find some common, civily indifferent but yet edifying ground. Yess mathematics.

"Think of what it would be like," I said, "if a man could jump as well as a grasshopper. That'd far out, wouldn't it?"

Ruth wanted to be helpful."Yeah, I suppose so."

"I'd like to figure it out," I said. "How far would it be. Let's see. Check it out. A grasshopper can jump 30 feet. And, let's say, they are about 4 inches long..."

I put my hands together, with about 4 inches between the index fingers. And began gyrating around as if I were a computer and the numbers of the calculation were running through me.

"So damn...that's ...30 times 12 ...that's 360 inches. And divided by 4 ...that's 90.

My eyes bugged open at the realization that the calculation had led me too, like a light going off inside my head.

"The grasshopper can jump 90 times their own body length!"

Ruth and Rose and her boyfriend began to look at each other and at me as if I has gone "over the edge."

I held out my hands, upturned like the Lord casting a blessing on the sea of fishes.

"Imagine how far a human being could jump," I said, "if you could jump 90 times your own body length. How many feet would that be?"

I struck the pose of the thinking man. I rested my chin on my thumb, my index finger covering my lips.

"Let's see," I said "Check it out. Let's say it's a 6 foot man. That's 6 x 90, that's 540 feet. Damn. That's almost two football fields! And there are 5,280 feet in a mile, so that's almost a tenth of a mile. Let's see there's about 10 city blocks in a mile, so it's one city block!

"A man who could leap one city block!

"Wouldn't that be marvelous."

I moved my hand in a long arch across the patio, made a sshheuuu sound like a jet.

"I'd like to hijack a grasshopper," I repeated, "and take it joy riding through the summer hiss. It would be like traveling on the moon.

The two women and the man, gazed at me wondering what I will do next. Ruth, trying to be supportive, agreed, tentatively, "That'd be a great way to get around, wouldn't it? Carrying your pack shopping and just jump a block at a time."

"Yeah, " someone else said.

"OK," I said, satisfied at the response. "Well how high would I have to jump to go a city block? ...You'd probably have to go up at least a hundred feet. My god that's 10 stories! You'd be like super-man able to leap over small buildings in a single bound — with ease!"

I clasp my arms around himself and moved villainously, stealth-ily stealing, carrying something off.

"I'd like to hijack a grasshopper and take it joy riding. It would be like traveling on the moon. You'd be almost free of gravity. You couldn't really tell ...how fine it was, with those big old clunky suites that the astronauts wore ...how fine it was ...to move in zero G."

I began crabbing, waffling, hedging around the patio as though buoyant, but also staggering as though weighted down. Ruth and Rose and her boyfriend laughed at my exaggerated Ralph Norton

100

moves.

"Imagine how fun," I continued, "my commute would be. It would be like Grasshopper Man goes down town."

I looked over at the almost finished sculpture, Big G, leaning against the house. I gestured toward it.

"There he is! Grasshopper Man, looking down on the world from his towering perch—any ledge or fire escape. I could leap down and commit a crime and leap away before anybody saw me."

I had them laughing pretty good at my antics by now. I was hamming it up, made a furtive motion, like a criminal fleeing the scene of the crime.

"I want to hijack a grasshopper and use it in my morning commute! I'd do these giant leaps, bounding from street to street moving through the city, or perhaps light on a balcony, in the Monday morning sunlight filtering through the haze."

I squatted down, ready to leap.

"You'd see me tuck into this incredible energy and leap across the horizon!"

I swirled around making highly exaggerated motions of a bow moving across the strings of a violin.

"I'd like to ride a grasshopper," I said, "take it out in the morning, keep it all day, play some tunes with the boys. I'd bow my fiddle with such vigor, I'd create a wall of white noise."

I cupped my hands over ears.

"Listen." I said. "Listen ...to the white noise wall ...of cicada sound."

It had never been so intense.

I stretched out my wrists like I was conducting an orchestra. I conducted. Then I made a gesture like a band leader introducing the rest of my sidemen, pointing to the insect musicians out in the field.

"I'd become a great player in the background hiss of summer. We'd be looking for the resonance frequency of summer in the harmonics of its heat! Looking all the way back to the fundamental frequency of the heat: the background heat, left over from the Big Bang! *Yeah*, man!"

I felt the white noise cicada sound...washing ...over me and I was being carried along in it. It poured through ... was filtered down ... became ameliorated.

"Listen." I said.

I cupped my hand over my right ear.

"That shifting chattering hiss of the summer cicadas sound. ...It's that fizz ...like that white noise between the channels on TV. ...Except this one goes up and down and shifts in and out."

I threw up my hands in triumph.

"It's modulated!"

I gazed at Ruth.

"Did you know," I asked her, "that white noise buzz you hear, when you change channels, is the background noise left over from the Big Bang?!"

Ruth smiled uncomfortably at Rose and her boyfriend.

"No," she said. "No I didn't know that."

They all looked at me weirdly. This made me defensive.

"Yeah that's right."

The peyote was really starting to come on me. The wall of cicada sound was getting intense. I could hear throbbing ...beats ...from the interference pattern of sounds coming from different sources crossing ...back and forth across me.

I did a defensive martial arts posture. Then like I was handling a huge ball, lifted my hand high above my head.

Ruth and Rose and her boyfriend were looking at me, bewildered, wondering what next.

I got this horrible feeling I was talking crazy, over their heads. It's just theater, I assured himself. I went into a kind of sing-songy Chinese opera voice with Tai Chi moves.

"There, I've said it twice, I'll say it again: The cicadas song is a harmonic of the white noise sound ... floating ...ubiquitously throughout the universe, left over by the Big BANG!"

As I said the word bang, I brought my hand down hard from on high and drove the heel into the palm of my other upturned hand, sliding it past wavered horizontally indicating the horizon. I had seen movies Tibetan monks using this gesture for the emphasis of driving home a fundamental point of philosophy.

"We are swimming in the ocean of space," I said, "being washed over by waves of the white noise of the universe."

I was going out of himself, and following the flow down a stream ...the wash would be concentrated into a stream of burbling ...white noise, but it was being filtered down, made sharper, into the cicada sound. It was what happened to me when I did Tai Chi, only more so.

"You can watch it on TV, too, you know," I said, knowing I was losing them. "Or pick it up on the radio. It is the universe outside the *window.*

At the word *window* I started flopping around, acting like I had gone into some kind of paroxysm of divine intervention. I tried to roll my eyes back up inside my head for good effect and in general acted like I was having an epileptic fit of insight. That got their attention, it certainly got mine. I was thinking of a window beyond our senses.

"You've seen it," I said, "that burbling white noise between channels, that snow. That's your TV picking up the background radiation of space!

"I don't have a TV," Ruth said.

"Neither do I," said Rose.

"But you've seen it haven't you," I said, "the electric jelly beans, between the channels."

"Yeah" Ruth said.

"But, so what?" said Rose, getting exasperated

"Well it's white noise," I argued, "and that's what these crickets and grasshoppers do. They channel the white noise of the universe! Grasshoppers study the secret of the universe by vibrating harmonically with the background Hissss of space."

I paused and looked at them, to see if they were getting it.

"Their trilling beats with it."

I presented my hands outstretched, like a lawyer resting his case before a jury.

"That's the secret of the Cicada's Song."

I paused, raised and lowered my eyebrows giving them a big simple moon face to see if any of this was making sense. "The background hiss of summer, *is* crickets and grasshoppers looking for the resonance frequency of summer, so that they can resonate with it and transmit a message through the background radiation of the universe to other planets!"

They all laughed.

"Yeah, RRRRight." someone said.

I started stumbling, acting like a blind man feeling his way, moving my hands back and forth in front of me.

104

"They are probing the space looking for the resonance frequency of summer by trying all these frequencies, forming these beats that get closer and closer to it. Listen!"

It was like the crickets and cicadas were sending out sound currents toward each other, moving in and out of the beats sending soundshapes Doppler-shifting around in the air.

I was swirling and doing a kind of Tai Chi pointing to the players, re-acting so fast that it looks like I is conducting them.

"The different groups of cicadas over here are pulsing groups of cicadas over THERE. And above it all are little high pitched cricket chirps on top of everything."

Then all of sudden they all stopped at once. A great silence fell over the proceeding like somebody had turned the sound off.

"Thank god!" exclaimed Ruth.

"Yeah, thank God, Jesus." Rose chimed with exaggerated relief like she was at an old time prayer meeting.

"Amen," said her boyfriend

"Listen to that silence," I managed to squeeze in, just as the great choir was starting up again, "you know how when one grasshopper stops another begins, ..."

Then all of sudden, the group was treated to another great silence. It was one of those unspoken things, one of those perfect moments when the universe conspired with the improvisational.

"...it is in those brief silences," I continued, taking advantage of the moment, "between when one quits and the next one begins, that a grasshopper is able to send a message to other planets through the background radiation of space."

"Woo, dude," said Rose's boyfriend Mark.

"Yes! It's true," I continued, acting oblivious to their teasing.

"Cicadas give off radio frequencies too. I've been able to pick it up on my radio when they buzz close to the fence antenna. And they get those radio frequencies that they generate to resonate with the background hiss of summer!"

They were looking at me as if I was completely, irrecoverably gone.

"That's right," I say smiling, shining them on in their incredulity. "We'd have to lead the radio listeners on a tour of the Radio Dude Ranch of the Air and describe what they are hearing."

"Listen," I said.

"Listen. It seems the beats are getting closer and closer together. A crescendo! They are coming together around something!"

In the heat and peyote I sensed the movement of Heat as an invisible mirage, moving across the landscape or a great Sky Being—this Energy, emerging out of the sound symphony. The millions of little beings in the field were like a pack of hounds or some kind of time animals chasing this Energy along with their sounds, like their sound beams were a web, to delineate and capture it. I got this image of them trying to grab Summer by the neck and make it stay with them a little longer, slow it down, to hug it, to hold it to them, to not let it slip through so fast. Summer is going by with a pack of hounds hanging on Him laughing and playing a game running through the fields.

"It's like an invisible mirage, moving across the landscape," I said, "Heat waves are its baton and it conducts this choir of crickets and grasshoppers."

"It's the wind!" I said throwing my hands in the air and twirling around. "The breeze—carries this invisible conductor striding, and here I did a tour jeté across the patio, "through the fields, and wherever he moves, the mirage of his presence is reconstructed in sound by the little animals stridulating where the heat is standing!"

I began walking around explaining things to them as if I were a CEO or marketing manager meeting in a boardroom. "That's what we'd do at the Radio Dude Ranch of the air. Fish for sounds! With our microphone balloons! Instead of having singing around the camp fire we'd ... we'd have group monkey chanting with the cicadas. They'd all be singing the cicada song and learning its secret.

"The kids of Camp Katydid would learn to harmonize with the heat. If you can't beat the heat you may as well join it. Maybe the kind of noise the cicadas make is like dogs panting to dissipate heat.

Ruth and Rose and Mark were getting kind of excited, maybe it was a kind of contact paranoia, but their eyes were bright and shining now, and I wanted to trust them even more.

"I want to show you a discovery I've made," I said.

With the superhuman strength of one high on adrenaline and peyote, I went inside, got the tape recorder and quickly carried it out and set it up on the table. I ran back and connected it to a 25 foot orange extension cord.

"Check it out," I said as I turned the tape player on.

"You know those recordings I made of the grasshopper a while back? Well listen to what they sound like when I play it back at half speed. Listen to this."

With a click I switched to a lower speed. "Listen. They are saying:
```
(((sex(((((xxx)))))sex)))
(((sex(((((xxx)))))sex)))
(((sex(((((x@x)))))sex)))
(((sex(((((x@x)))))sex)))
```
"They are *not*," Ruth teased.

"Yes they are," I insisted. "Listen, here's what it sounds like real, and here's what it sounds like slowed down," I flipped the switch, changing the speeds a couple of times. "They are saying:

```
(((sex(((((xxx)))))sex)))
(((sex(((((xxx)))))sex)))
(((sex(((((x@x)))))sex)))
(((sex(((((x@x)))))sex)))
```

clear as a bell."

"Hmmm. Well, damn. It does sound like that," Ruth mused.

"Grasshoppers are obsessed with sex," I argued. "They are multiplying fiendishly out there in my patch right now as we speak."

For a moment, the company all just seemed to sit there listening to them eating my crops.

"Imagine that," I said, breaking the lull. "being able to follow the heat through the fields, to kind of surf on its wavering motion as it changes the air."

By now the cicadas were bearing me out, as if I could some how control them with my mind, like the way you can, if you are on acid and at a Grateful Dead concert outside and you feel like you and Jerry are moving the clouds across the sun with his guitar.

It was a marvelous texture, the swirling, shifting white noise with the cicada trilling pattern in it. I turned to Ruth and Rose and Mark and said, "Let's chant along with it."

It was a broiling hot summers day, and Ruth and Rose and her boyfriend thought, 'What the hell'.

I waved my hands like a conductor, "Breathe in.

"Breathe out.

"With a long easy white noise sound ...shhhh ...hhhaaaa."

I moved my hands, palms toward me, drawing sound out of them.

"Let's sing along, breathe in, make the white noise, say it loud, say it strong, say it long, "Sex, listening in, listening in, space in the sky of sex x sex, sex sexsex, sex sexsex,

```
(((sex(((((xxx)))))sex)))
(((sex(((((xxx)))))sex)))
(((sex(((((x@x)))))sex)))
(((sex(((((x@x)))))sex)))
```

And they answered, feebly at first. "Sex, sex sex sex, sex sex."

And I started winding up like a preacher, "And when you get hundreds and thousands saying this in groups that's probably where the word Sex came from."

I shrugged my shoulders, threw my hands up in the air at the inevitable conclusion, "Grasshoppers are obsessed with sex."

"Sex sex, sex sex sex, sex sexsex, sex," they began chanting, louder and louder, really getting into it.

Well. It was about that time that I really started losing it. I had to do something to top all this holding forth. What better way than to go mad.

"I gonna go out into the field," I said. "I'll start directing the grasshoppers."

There I was, shifting back and forth from the crickets and cicadas in the field to the chorus of people, from real cicada sound to slower speed white noise sex sound—back and forth—moving to different localizations in space.

"OK, some of you say it soft," I said, directing the fields.

"And some of you over here say it loud," I said, directing in the other direction

"SEX SEX SEX," chanted the chorus of Ruth, Rose and the boyfriend.

"OK, now you over there!" I said pointing at another part of the field. I yelled, "Stop!"

And they did!!

"God, isn't that amazing when they all stop at once," I said to the group.

And then an amazing thing happened, one part stops dead silent while another group starts up on the other side.

"We've got an antiphony going!" I exclaimed. "We got call and response going!

"Sky God!

"Ring crickets, play piccolos cicadas, wildly, trill grasshoppers whistle, trill endlessly, expand!"

I began to direct by moving my hands in waves across the fields

"OK, now lets see if I can get them to do an echo," I said, "across the landscape from loud to soft, like a wave."

And they did. The cicada sound was moving across the land-scape underneath a sinusoid amplitude envelope.

"Oh, Great Sky Being," I intoned, "He is moving among you. Chase him with your songs!"

My friends were laughing. Nervously.

"Now move the sound up and down," I continued to conduct, "as if playing with gravity."

And then they all could really hear it clearly. It was as if the cicadas were showing them the elements of their symphony: the high crickets are really the second harmonic and the cicadas are the third and highest harmonic, all playing off the fundamental, the wind and the burbling white noise.

"Yes, listen it's moving, in, over there! It's moving up and down. Yes!

110

•••

His Eyes Turned Topaz

While we continued to worry about the plague, Big G—the giant heavy metal Grasshopper—became as tall as the house. The two eyes were huge. They looked like the bubble eyes of a helicopter. Ruth had wanted them to be in a place where they were hit directly by the morning sun. The beast was oriented due east.

There was a lot of copper ducting on it too, which she got from an old cotton mill that they were taking down, and glad to get rid of. So the grasshopper had this cupric green kind of waxy sheen to it. The bubble eyes and the leather skin tubing of its thorax fitting in between the arches of the slide made it look like a small helicopter with hind legs.

She made a giant grasshopper out of that thing.

You could actually get inside the eyes, and look out through the faceted lenses, some parts clear and some parts many-colored and like a metal colander grown large with that many holes but the holes were larger and plugged with pure-colored glass.

It was the way the head flowed into the thorax, through this gathered distressed leather that really made it look real. She got a grinder and a sander and sanded down some parts of the copper so that these shined brilliantly.

It was a 10-foot tall, 19-foot long grasshopper!

She got it to be big enough so that a person could crawl inside and get behind the eyes and look at all these pure lights, red and green and purple. You could see through the bits of colored glass with enough acuity to make out shapes, through the many faceted eyes.

There it was. Finished. A kind of half metal, half leather-and-glass creature. Huddled by the back porch on the patio. One look at this thing and you could tell that it was the creation of a demented mind infected with genius. The parts fit so well together that they looked like they were destined to come together, and that the creature was dreaming about metamorphosing into something else, an ever further far out being.

"This is it," she said.

16

WITHIN A BUDDING GROOVE

It was August in Texas, and some days it was so hot that the birds went on strike and refused to fly. When a dog chased a rabbit, they both walked. All the pot plants had long since dropped off their big baby fan leaves, taken on secondary growth, and a couple of months after the sun reached its zenith at solstice, had begun to flower. Time goes by so teasingly slow for the small time farmer, waiting for his pot plants to show forth their sex, that when sexual maturity finally does occur, it is a blessed relief.

By now the patch was safe from locusts. Greg and I had put way more than enough plants out there to survive the onslaught. Even the taciturn Greg had to acknowledge one day, "Jesus Christ! We've got one hell of a lot of marijuana growing out here!"

The second-wave planting had caught up with the first, and was starting to bud too. The cicada choppers had, in fact, served as a severe cut-back machine — cutting away the lower and inside sucker leaves that didn't get that much light anyway. This had helped the surviving plants become broad and bushy.

The patch was like a very big Christmas tree lot filled to capacity, the trees so close they touched each other. When you walked among them you had to part them to move through. There was enough for everybody. Little Thais with their delicate turned up leaves. Tall Colombian beauties, bronzed Hawaiians.

Cigars

Greg and I still inspected each plant closely to make sure there wasn't any sex reversal and to pinch off the primary leaves which they just dropped on the ground in a ring around the plant for mulch. Some of the big fan leaves Gregory preserved to later use in making big hand-rolled marijuana cigars.

Greg, doing his best imitation of the fat-cat redneck said: "I'm gonna use some of these big fan leaves to make a big ole fat marijuana cee-gar. One that don't even have any paper to get between you and the smoke."

Each cigar had about as much bud as a Thai stick. Watching Greg's hands at work was like watching an expert fisherman tie flies. Greg made a kind of paper out of the leaves by interleaving them in opposite directions and sticking their edges together with a bead of sticky, amber-colored hash oil which he had to heat up in a double boiler to make flow.

"When the crop comes in," said Greg, "we'll have to make up a batch of this hash oil. It is quite an involved process with screens and double boilers and chemicals and it is very wasteful. You have to have a lot of weed."

Then Greg rolled up the crushed and cleaned marijuana flowers into the green fan leaf which made the outer skin of the cigar. When it was rolled up tight, he sealed the flap with another bead of hash oil and a lick. He held it for several minutes waiting for the cigar to dry. He gently set aside the masterpiece to admire it. These feats of manual dexterity and perspicuity amazed me.

To store these excellent hand-rolled marijuana cigars, Greg bought a box of long cylindrical vials—the kind that expensive Cuban cigars come in—with the humidor cap. There it was, a big green cigar. He was so proud of it, that he set up a photo shoot. Greg was like a diorama artist or a *mise en scene* master. He laid out a stacked of the cigars like they were trees in a lumber yard, near an ashtray that looked like a building. He tossed in a couple of the smaller green cheroots he had made, to make it look like a hurricane in a lumber yard. This was all under some noire looking lamp that Martin Scorsese might have used on the set in <u>Taxi Driver</u>. He took a whole role of Polaroid photos of it. He sent one anonymously to High Times magazine. I was shocked to actually come across the picture in the magazine several months later. It had a caption:

> "Rural Artisans bringing back the fine art of cigar making. These marijuana cigars are buds rolled up in a marijuana leaf paper and stuck together with hash oil."

The Texas Twister Hybrid

Gregory's special prized plants in the animal pens were really amazing. One of the hybrids, *the Creature in the Hog Pen*, which we now had begun calling *Big Bertha*, had a whole hog pen for herself. She had become a big ungainly thing, draping herself out like a kind of may pole, each of the four main side branches that had been stretched and trained extending out and away from the central stock running along the wires for ten feet in all directions. "This is what the French call *espalier* to the max," Greg said, with a smile of satisfaction.

I wanted to know the formula for the seed stock of this gangly hybrid. It was outrageous to look at it, even the side leaves were studded with tiny little glistening drops of THC. I said: "I'd sure like to know what plants you mixed together to get this here Texas Twister hybrid," indicating the ungainly creature in the hog pen.

"Texas Twister hybrid, ha ha, that's pretty good," Greg laughed. "You like it, don't you?

"Yeah." I said, my eyes lighting up with enthusiasm.

"Texas Twister. That's a good name for it. Because it really is almost a vine."

"Well I can tell you this, he said smugly, it's a multiple hybrid, —at least a 3-way hybrid — and it's the result of many years scientific breeding."

"Multiple hybrid, what is that?"

"Well, duh. Didn't you study that in biology?" he said taking his usual pre-instructional umbrage. "It takes, of course," (and he looks at me as if to say, you idiot), "2 generations. You start off with 3 batches of seeds. The first generation you grow two kinds of seeds. When these mature you let them cross pollinate. Then you take the seeds from this union and plant them for the 2nd generation. This is now hybrid one. You also plant the 3rd bunch of seeds. And then when these plants grow up and you cross pollinate them. Then the seeds they produce are your 3-way hybrid."

"Now when you plant those seeds," he continued, "you should get a mixture of some of the best traits of all three—or you can also get the worst. That's why it's real important to keep the book."

"And, I can tell you this," he said. It combines 3 of the strongest varieties known to man."

"Don't tell me now. Let me guess."

"OK."

"If I'm right let me know."

"OK"

"Well first off, it would have to be some plants from India."

"Right." Greg nodded his head in appreciation of my growing sophistication.

"And then it would have to be maybe a Hawaiian or a Tai."

"Well, hmmm, Yes," he hedged.

He was not being all that forthcoming.

"Come on Greg, don't make me beg, what is the formula."

And then he said something that made me really sad: "I'm not sure I'm going to tell you. Maybe I should just keep it as a trade secret, like the secret formula for Coca Cola."

I just felt totally untrusted.

"Yea, right, I said, defensive. "I'd like to see you register that with the fed."

He turned away from me,

The name Texas Twister stuck.

I wanted to get the breeding formula for these seeds, so that I could go off on my own. By now I felt like I had found my calling; Outlaw growing was quite a rush. It's not that I had an ulterior motive, we were partners (in crime!) and I just wanted to know if the results are repeatable. After all I had named it. I talked to him as much as I could. He relented and finally gave it out. He said: "Well, it was just my good luck to find it. At first I thought it was some kind

116

of weakling because of the way it falls over and droops down, but if you grow it on supports it does really well.

"It was just an accident really, I was trying all kinds of cross pollination. What I do is collect pollen from males by shaking their branches in a closed room over a plastic bag. And then I suck up the pollen into a turkey baster. Then I cover a branch of the female, in another room, with a clear plastic bag. I tie it off at both ends, and then using the turkey baster with a bulb, send a big blast of male pollen all over the flowers of the female.

"This growing indoors is OK for producing seed stock, but I'm really glad to be growing this one, the Texas Twister hybrid as you call it, on the outside, where it will get the wind and the air and the real sun.

"It produces what I call the halo stone."

"Halo stone. What do you mean by that," I asked.

"Well, maybe you can come up with a better word for it, but when I used pollen from Panama Red on flowers from Thailand, the plants I got were exceptionally clear in the stone they provided.

"It was just an idea I got from those holy pictures we used to have in Catholic school. You know, how people got light coming out of 'em. This weed seems to put a glow around everything like that. Anyway, you'll find out."

And that's as close to the truth as I got. I think the Texas Twister hybrid was a 3-way hybrid: from some tall Indian ganesh, a rangy Tai, and the glistening Panama Red. But who knows where that Red jumped ship from in Panama, or about the years, maybe centuries of breeding that had gone on in India.

The name of the Rose

I was getting into naming the plants. I started calling one, *the Bride*, because she had clusters of fine lacy white hairs growing all out of her flowers. It stood so tall, you could see it from anywhere in the garden. We had *Hawaiian Beauty* next to *Thai Cloud*, along with the traditional *Ganja Goodie*, and *Panama Red*.

Cool, Mellow, Dreamy, Greg and I were thinking of all kinds of highs. It seemed the naming of marijuana flowers would not have so much to do with the blooming of them and how they looked, as with the kind of high that you got from them, or expected to get.

I appreciated Greg's hands-on approach; Greg's knowledge was real, not nominal like my own. Greg, though sometimes embarrassed, had to smile at my way with words. We got into a typical discussion over the naming of one plant that I had started calling *Amitaba*. I sometimes referred to the same plant simply as *Her Grace*.

Greg was always competitive, had the 'if not invented here, it's no good attitude'. "I've got a better name for it," he insisted. He paused for effect: "Einstein."

"Einstein, that *is* pretty good," I agreed, "but I like *Amitaba* better."

"Amitaba," Gregory repeated blankly. "What's that mean?"

"It comes from the Tibetan. 'Amitaba was its grace'. Amitaba is a kind of wet light. (Tibetan mysticism is sort of a hobby of mine.)"

"Wet light!" Gregory shook his head in derision. "What the hell does that mean? That doesn't make any sense to me."

"O you know," I tried to explain, "light from under water, the light that goes off inside your head when you understand something. Insight."

118

"Well why don't you just call it *Insight* then."

"Yeah, that's a good one. We'll call one of them that too."

"Well, you make up all the names you want. I don't care. The main thing is, that we know their parentage."

•••

I felt really good. I had been working all summer doing hard physical labor. I had used the solitude to get further into yoga and Tai Chi. It was great to do cadas totally alone out in a vast panoramic open field. The sky was an upturned bowl, and I was a golem—the upright part of a sundial used to measure time. Turning and turning I was a shadow of the celestial turning of the earth. This was the summer of the hand stand. I got strong enough and got my balance up enough to be able to do a handstand. I could actually walk on my hands.

I thought I was becoming a man of knowledge. I was becoming more aware of the world. It was not the same kind of "paranoid" awareness and street smarts—being aware for example, to the slam of a car door or the comings and goings of the phone company that you get when you are a marijuana dealer, everybody has that because if you smoke you deal. This was different. I was becoming country wise.

Growing weed was turning out to be one of the best learning experiences I had ever had. Although I had been all through college, I had never really had the kind of hands-on learning experience that I was getting by apprenticing myself to a master grower. I was learning a lot about marijuana. I hoped it would become my new trade. There was lots of opportunity: hand rolled marijuana cigars and cheroots, oils and butters, not to mention fine smoking. Maybe even start dealing in hemp futures. This was before computers. I, like many hopeful striving but under-achieving young men, thought the world was going over to an underground drug economy.

I had to admit that part of the pot plant's beauty was the money. Yes sir, this was a crop of money trees. We had some 200 plants that would each yield at least 10 ounces. That's 2000 ounces. Pot was selling for about $100 an ounce. That's $200,000 which, when you split it two ways is $100,000 dollars each. $100,000 was enough to get you started in the great game of life.

But more than the money, was the feeling that a deepening of consciousness was occurring in my mind. This was accompanied by a nagging fear and sometimes even despair that this new awareness, of being in the embrace of Summer, of being touched on the lips by the background kiss of summer, of being able to tune into the symphony of summer and to know the secret of the cicadas' song could only mean that I was slipping into madness.

•••

I was so proud of my new knowledge, I wanted to communicate with other growers and hybridizers. I was feeling a sense of community with farmers everywhere, in particular pot farmers.

I wondered what the other growers were like. Were they all like Greg, crotchety, perfectionistic. Explosive abusive, but really just a very devoted person at heart. I wanted another opinion about my growing knowledge.

My only other experience with growers had been a growing co-op that Sue had introduced me to in Vermont. That was when I was with Sue, the girl from Montreal. Sue picked me up when I was hitchhiking through Vermont. The affair that changed my life had begun when this groovy country woman picked up this striking,

120

long-haired man standing by the side of the road hitchhiking in rural eastern Quebec. In order to be with Sue, I stayed in the community she lived in across the boarder in Vermont for a while. It was after the end of the growing season and we somehow got up into an abandoned bus on a farm. The bus was used as a processing and cleaning center to package the local home grown. I was surprized to find how well organized the growing community was. Those country folks trusted each other. On the bus I saw tables where piles of marijuana colas had been trimmed by local workers previously in the day. The floor of the bus was covered with leaf and shake, apparently to be swept away. They packaged the buds in large burlap feed sacks which I saw stacked like at a produce depot. Those Vermonters are serious growers, I thought. They are mild-mannered country people who get up early in the morning and go to church. They are strong American people, wearing glasses, flannels and beards standing in their freedom gardens reveling in the glory of their buds.

Well, I didn't know. The only *other* hybridizer I ever knew was my own grandfather. All of a sudden I decided to start writing letters to my old grandfather. I was dying to share this new knowledge with someone to whom I thought it would matter. The last time I had seen Bapa was when the old boy threw me out of the house. The grandfather had seen me, with my long hair at the time, going up the stairs from behind. The old man had become confused, and thought I was bringing a girl up to my room!

The old boy was way up into his 90's but still got dressed up every day in his tweeds, with a white permanent press shirt, and a tie, and walked through the small, tree-shrouded New England town by a river he had lived in all his life, to get the mail or down to the docks to buy a fish. I picture him puttering around among his trellises of roses, and I hoped that longevity was his legacy to me.

I wanted to talk to this rose fancier about being accepted. I started wanting to reach across generations somehow, to go back to a time when men felt a part of the earth. I wanted to say I shared their knowledge and work ethic, I wanted to be accepted in the larger context, accepted by someone in my own family, somebody who had written me off as hopeless. I wanted to talk to the older generation and say it meant a lot to us what you did and we are carrying on the tradition.

So, I decided to write a letter to my grandfather, casually asking technical questions about bloom blushers and soil acidity, then slip in a question about the naming conventions of roses. Maybe we could share the quest for the perfect varietal. I had to construct a language that was at once scientific and metaphorical. This use of euphemisms is an art among old dopers. On the phone, people say, "I got those three types of music you were interested in. I'll have to bring them over and play them for you." It is always best to be paranoid; phones aren't secure.

> Dear Grandfather,
> I have been getting into growing roses down here in Texas.
> I've got a good garden. I was wondering about bloom enhancers or blushers, fertilizing compounds that you can put on roses to make them bloom better.
> I know that you have hybridized roses, and I wonder about the naming convention. I know you named the ones you hybridized after Queen Elizabeth, but do these have to be officially recognized by the "American Rose Growers" associations.
> How do you get your name associated with them.
> Can you just name them the Walker Underwood Rose, or how distinct a varietal do they have to be.

The old boy wrote back! With advice on bloom blushers, from phosphorous to nitrogen. I thought that since weed and roses were both climbers and liked the same kind of light and soil, that this might be good advice. I brought these suggestions up to Gregory.

"Naw. No way," Greg said. "We want to use something organic. Those rose growers don't have to worry about how things taste. We do."

With a derisive chuckle he added, "No dice, Charley. We want to grow tunas that taste good, not tunas with good taste."

•••

I wished we had a tradition of Marijuana Grower's Associations. Yeah right, that'd be highly likely. Instead I turned to rose fanciers to fill this need to talk to other growers. I wanted to find out how they named their hybrids.

I went to a rose show in Austin. I wanted to rub shoulders with hybridizers. I felt weird in it, like I was giving in to some kind of awful compunction or need for human connection. I crabbed, waffled, and hedged my way around the periphery just trying to see what these people were about. I felt like I was in some kind of Clint Eastwood movie. I imagined the marijuana growers—grizzled, wearing serapes and bandoleeros, bearded and burnt from weeks out in the bush, smoking dark cigarillos—strolling menacingly among the little, balding, croquet playing, crumpet eating, rose growers who did not dare to even look in our direction, let alone look down their noses at us.

The marijuana growers would have some legitimate name like the American Marijuana Association, the AMA. They brought their finest flowers to the showdown and discussed them technically with other growers. In my fantasy, I imagined Gregory and me being honored at the flower show. The judges talked us up before the assemblage saying: "They are hybridizers in the service of our generation, preserving exotic varietals and producing new ones." I even gave a paper as Dr. Walker Underwood titled something like "Prolegomena for the future of mind/body therapies" in which I presented a proposal for developing strains of weed that are targeted at specific ailments. Like one kind good for glaucoma, might not be the best for wasting syndrome, or bipolar temperament. It ended with a note on the economic window: "In spite of all the current paranoia the situation has an upside: the government is providing us with the invaluable service of annihilating foreign competition, thus helping us create a monopoly on the domestic market." The pot growers showed off plants with Latinate names like *Texas Twistorium* and *eplurabus hmmm*, etc. Of course, in addition to smell and taste, there is a whole other dimension to the flowering of marijuana that is not even visible. Marijuana flowered in the dimension of the mind. I tried to imagine a show that displayed not only Maryjane's botanical beauty but also her psychobotanical beauty as well.

•••

I wrote a poem to my grandfather about the flowering of the rose that really reflected what was going on in my mind, but of course never sent it to my grandfather, nor showed to anyone. It was a mystical reflection on the opening of a rose, and a contrast between physical beauty and psychobotanical beauty — the rose gives us its visual beauty but Maryjane flowers in the brain — kind of idea.

The Unfolding.
When the rose is unfolding
deploying

124

unpacking
itself
 into the symmetry of its petals
we can see that the petals
those light-binding diaphanous sheets
of the most marvelous velvet color
fling themselves out and settle down over a life force
which shows itself as radiating out
in all directions
centrifugally
from the central fugue of its moving center.

O God no, I thought, he'll never get that—something is in a
fugue state dreaming the rose into existence

However, I continued,

The rose stands there like a representation of multidimensional
space, her center
unfolding
pregnant with perfume slowly drifting
 off on the eddies of air
her flowering unfolds like a smile
her memories full of rain
and the nourishment of good ground
she is probably a beacon of light
in the infrared skyways of the insects

Ah well, what I was trying to express to the old guy was something about this abstract life force. I pictured it from non-Euclidean
mathematics as a curved surface whose shape was similar to the
shape of a rose, interleaved, discontinuous surfaces of local space

time were like the petals. This archetypal space time surface of the universe shows itself most clearly in the rose, but also shows itself in the brain flower, the discontinuous leaps of thought. The rose flowers in a space of visual beauty; pot flowers in an inside space of physical feeling — the brain.

Moving through the surface of the high was like moving through the surface of a flower that was unfolding itself in the brain. It was like that fine velvety fuzzy fizz on the surface of a rose petal was a soft tongue caressing that brain like it was a tongue or a pair of lips.

The high is like being on interspersed sheaths of space-time, with discontinuous leaps from one surface to another and each surface is velvet. Moving through this velvet color is like being imbued with a slowed-down perception, somehow the filters are stopped up with the resiny oil — light moves slowly through so that you can hear your own mind working, hear it thinking about all kinds of things. Watch it move along dynamic lines of force across generations through your own psychology.

The inner surface of the marijuana high is as light as smoke, as if the drifting smoke were a kind of moving flower, with ever shifting petals slipping up vertical...

The Perfect Moment

Greg and I were really on a roll. Hybrids, clones, espalier to the max. We worked and watched and waited for the perfect moment when the flowers would be ripe and at their peak. We inspected them closely. The Perfect Moment was when these gooey little tendrils shooting out of the flower, have matured to the point where it is half fresh and half starting to turn from a clear or white to red and gold. The oil spreads out from floral cluster and explodes from there and

126

goes all up and down the leaf, sprinkling itself like bursts of pixie dust on the inner leaves around it.

We harvested the flowers individually at first. We took a floral cluster usually about as big as your thumb when it was right, when the number of red was equal to the number of clear or milky white. We took the whole cluster, because it is good protection for the flower to have its shade leaves around it. Then, when a whole branch more or less reached that perfect moment, when about half of the little hairs had turned color we took the whole branch. These would later be trimed for smoking.

17

SWIMMING IN THE DARK

There was some wild land out there—a ways off—on somebody else's property. It was across the fence and beyond the tree line. I would sneak onto the land and go swimming in this big pond—tanks they are called. I never saw anybody else out there, day or night. It was especially wild to go swimming in the dark. It had been fenced in for a long time. Cows had never been in there. It looked different from the other land around it because it still had the native mesquite and cactus growing on it. I thought the swimming hole was a sink-hole into the aquifer, because there was some rock around it and it didn't go dry all summer even though there was a drought.

The water was cool and refreshing, a welcome respite in the heat.

It was August in Texas and each day was broiling, the nights not much better. During the day, the heat was so astounding and the cicadas were so intense that it just fried your brain and left you in soporific stupor, unable to think or move. But then I thought about how all this heat sweats the THC out of the plants and I didn't mind it so bad. I'd be thinking about taking a dip all the time, and slipped away whenever possible.

The pond had to be approached with caution and ritual. Caution because it was just me way out in the night, sneaking onto another man's land and ritual because I thought of it as the ritual bath of the warrior. It was really a trip to walk around on wild land at night. Some nights the stars were so clear you could see the whole cross section of the Milky Way and it was so dark that you felt like you might walk off the edge of this world into those stars.

Well, of course, Butch was there—off to the side, watching me. Silent, fast, totally aware, Butch was a medicine dog, watching over me.

"Come on Butch, you want to go for a ...walk?"

Butch's eyes would light up at the sound of that word.

"I ought to go out and check the plants now, see how they are doing. They are so beautiful I can't keep away.

"But maybe we should go down to the pond for a swim. It's been a long hot day."

I looked out into the black and luminescent moonscape of the land. "Which way will we go tonight?"

Ah, for the life of a country gentleman. Life was simple. The only question I had to answer for the evening's activity was should I go left or should I go right for my evening stroll. Leaving from the patio I might either follow the brick path to the left back behind the house, past the well, and move in the shadows of the enormous tree. It looked over us, by day like some giant protective being, distributing its shadows for us to seek cool in, and by night stretching up its twig tips into the dark, pulling down moon shadows for us to dance in. And continuing, move on past the garden to the hidden entrance to the secret path back to the patch. Or I could choose to go the other way, past the hog pens over the fence, along the tree line, down the dry creek to the pool. Such were the choices of the country gentleman.

I liked to go alone. There was something about going on these midnight swims that I had to do alone as a kind of ninja training. I had always been a master of stealth, *el hombre invisible* and had that kind of Mr. Unemployed ...Mr. Gray ...I'm-with-the-band, kind of hanging back in the shadows ability ever since I learned how to cruise through school. I wasn't just sneaking onto some guy's property to go swimming in my tank at night, it was more like stalking. I was not stalking anything in particular, it was stalking in the sense of filling this place with your awareness, so that nothing went on around you that you didn't know about. Although I did take Ruth there sometimes during the day, at night I got into a kind of stalking behavior so I never took Ruth for a moonlight swim because you had to be focused.

To get there I'd go through the trees, down the tree line and along the dry creek. I'd go quiet as the breeze, because you never knew when somebody might be—watching you—onto another man's land. The trick was to be invisible and be the one watching them.

Going there was like walking onto a piece of ancient land, a place before crops, before man ever walked around here. It was like going onto the land that time forgot. Crickets and frogs doing their summer symphony got louder and louder as Butch and I got closer to the pond. You had to sneak up on them too, didn't want to disturb, be noticed, come up on some redneck, get killed.

Over the fence and down the dry creek bed in the moonlight. The plants that grew on the banks of the dry creek bed had been thinned out by the drought and they spangled the moon glow on their leaves. I am moving down the silver moon stones of a dry creek in the moonlight. The dry creek was a ritual walk for me to descend. The forest was opalescent in the lunar light. Glowing and nacreous, like mushrooms living on dead things.

Very quietly there.

Might be eyes in the woods.

Why not.

There are your eyes.

Ahhh. Come to the ancient mesquite trees with their long claw-like pods drooping down over the pond.

Stand and watch for a while.

The black water quiet, undulating the reflected moon.

Butch still, knew we were stalking. He would bark and defend me if need be. The mesquite trees poised. A cloud floated slowly across the moon. As the silvery moon glow winked out, the clear night shadows turned into chiaroscuro, sheltering all into darkness.

Slipping out of clothes. Feel so vulnerable naked. Slipping into pond, quiet. Shock of water.

Floating on a pond in the dark. You've got to do it just right to get the effect. You want to get your ears under the water so that just your eyes and face are floating on the surface looking up beyond the forest; not getting any of the black night forest in your periphery. You

130

must adjust your float so there is no periphery, just you looking into the night, no edge, no point of reference, letting it all slip away.

I am floating on my back encased up to my face in black water. Just the slightest exertion necessary to keep the water from coming in over me, but at the same time keeping my eyes as close down to the surface so that I can't see the trees because then I felt that the whole earth was my eye. I was the artist, an antenna of the race, looking out into space and trying to receive the communication from other worlds.

I got a tunnel vision in which I was looking up at the night sky through a very wide tunnel as round as the pond. I saw himself as ...as just my face, filling out to the edges of the pond and it made the pond sort of a big fish eye lens. I realized that I could see myself from above, like I was floating over the land and the pond, floating several thousand feet above the pond looking back down at myself floating there in the center of the water, as if floating in an eye. I wondered what this projected astral body was, my *local spirit of place*, perhaps. But then instead of floating on the surface of the lens I would be this entity looking *through* the lens out millions and millions of miles up into the dark night sky and could see the stars were beacons of light, beckoning us to come out. I could see something, a shadow, a shape, a give-and-take between the point group of the stars on the celestial sphere and the deep spaces between them. It was just the universe—as ephemeral and as persistent as an abstraction can be. Yet somehow it held all the patterns of my life as seen from afar. Perhaps this was a *distant* projection of my astral body, my *remote spirit of place*. And yet I could sense these two states of being were linked by a long thin line, a double spiral long and winding and stretched thin as time. It was a glimpse of evolution linking these two states. States of me.

There I was, my good old lean and craggy countenance looking up an opening in the night. I had slipped my moorings, been cast away, been caught in the flow and looking up at the ever expanding outward-horizoning walls, asked myself: What am I *doing* out here.

But then I couldn't keep the water from rolling up around my eyes. It too is searching, watching and just as I was about to let myself feel the presence of other civilizations I sank back under it, lost the signal and felt at home in the water.

The Song of Maryjane

18

A POT RUSTLER INTERDICTION PROGRAM

By the end of August the patch was in full flower and Gregory and I worried about pot rustlers. Gregory kept talking about Ripoff, the person, as in: "We've got to set some kind of booby trap for Ripoff."

For Greg, Ripoff was some kind of heinous tobacco-spitting redneck white devil like those mountain retards in the movie *Deliverance*.

"The Ripoff might have a gun," he said looking me in the eye. "You never know what they might do to you out here. There's nobody around."

He got a panic stricken look on his face. "We've got to get something that is a strong deterrent."

"What would we do to him if we caught him?" I asked.

We looked at each other aghast. We didn't have an answer to this question. "We'll have to catch him first," Greg said.

"We could make a trap," he mused out loud. "We could make one like in Viet Nam, —a hole with sharpened sticks in the bottom of it, pointing up —pungie sticks. The hole would be covered with grass, so that Ripoff would fall in and become impaled on the sticks."

Talk like this from my partner made me paranoid. Gregory started buying back issues of *Soldier of Fortune* magazine from the

Half-Price Book Store on Lavaca Street. *High Times* magazine didn't mention what to do about pot rustlers; *Soldier of Fortune* did.

"This issue shows how to make booby traps," Greg said, pointing to a Soldier of Fortune cover. The cover showed the face of a soldier with black grease smeared under his eyes. The soldier in camouflage fatigues was peering out from behind bushes with the baleful stare of a war hardened idiot. Across the cover it read "My First 1,000 Yard Kill."

"Look at this," he said, slapping the magazine with the back of his hand, "They show how to make a pit with Punji sticks.".

I was really freaked out when Gregory showed me a booby trap he had actually gone ahead and built. "It's called 'A Poor Man's Land Mine', he said cackling to himself. "I built it in my shop."

It was a little wooden box with a circular hole drilled through the center of one side. A nail had been driven through the other side exactly opposite the center of the hole.

"You set a shotgun shell into the hole," he began.

He set the shotgun shell into the box pointing up so that the firing ring of the shotgun shell just rested on the nail.

"Now you bury this box in the ground," he said.

"The business end points up," he continued "This part you cover with a board." He bent over and covered the up-pointed shotgun shell with a board.

He held the board above the box. "If you step on the board," he said, "it pushes the shell into the nail and ka-blooie—it explodes.

"God damn!" I said aghast.

"Since there is no rifle barrel to channel the shot," he said, "it goes off in all directions." He shook his head in dismay and admiration at the device.

"Man that could really tear up somebody's leg," I said.

"Yea! That's the idea!" Greg said. "Teach them sons-a-bitches not to come 'round here. Ever."

He saw my wide eyed look of disbelief. "But it's not fatal," he quickly, added, making a mollifying gesture with his hand. "But it would definitely make it necessary for Ripoff and those in his tribe to get out of here in a hotfooted hurry!

At this he started doing a kind of a hotfooted dance, like a one-legged man dancing a jig. "They'd have to go immediately to a hospital," he said, cackling and twirling around.

I shook my head. "Gruesome business."

I talked my partner out of any of this stuff and we settled for stringing the grapefruit juice cans around the perimeter so that anyone moving through there would make a lot of noise. We also made a rule that one of us had to be out in the patch on sentry duty every night. Gregory started bringing his Dobermans out.

Gregory brought to camping the same kind of methodical zeal he brought to building. He set up an army surplus cot under a camou-flaged mosquito net in the shade of the old oak tree. He wore camou-flaged fatigues and a redneck bill cape with ACE lettered across its front. Gregory had the great Texas savvy of managing to avoid the heat by not working at the wrong time of the day. Yet he always seemed to be busy puttering, tweaking, polishing his binoculars, sharpening a knife. He was so methodical. He built a balance beam scale that was super accurate. We checked it against several in grocery stores. He built hiding holes for the various kinds of mush-rooms, peyote, speed and acid that were showing up at the farm. Some of these hidey holes were elaborate affairs with hidden drawers and false bottoms. I worried about him. Texas is a hot and hissing place. Gregory had a really red neck and seemed to have high blood pressure for one so young.

I started doing Tai Chi out in the patch as part of my anti-pot-rustler maintenance program. It made me feel totally competent and able to handle anything to be out there with my dog by my side keeping my watch underneath the stars. It was scary being out there all alone, but for the first time in my life I had hope. It looked like I was about to walk into a bright future with lots of money coming in and I did not want to see it ripped off. I wanted to be out there and be so quiet that I could make the wind my ally. I enjoyed being in a state of hyper awareness —due to a mixture of fear, marijuana and adrenaline, thrilling through my body, surging through the night air in every pull-back, push, dodge and parry. I did have some compunction about violating the sanctity of the Tai Chi head space by doing it stoned. I could see the lineage of Taoist saints shaking their heads in dismay at this infidel, who had been taught by a white former-Presbyterian minister in Berkeley.

You come to know the wind out here, when you live in the country, you become kin to the wind, listening in to everything coming because you don't want anything to come up and surprise you. Maybe it was paranoia, maybe feral sensitivity, but I became preternaturally aware while I was doing Tai Chi. I began to be able to use the wind as an ally for its ability to carry awareness. I discovered that sound can travel for miles and miles. If you can be still for a very long time — at least several hours — you can start to detect sounds from quite far away.

On one level Tai Chi is a trance-inducing shadow boxing dance. In the dark you box with the shadow side of your own nature. I would be out there on high alert doing the form in the pot patch. I'd look up at the surrounding wall of trees at the edge of the tallgrass fields, and see them leaning and moving together, like at the end of the movie *Blow Up* when the breeze was swashing and swaying in the trees, where it got into the existential conundrum and you kind of wanted to cry or jump for joy at the mystery of being, but you knew you couldn't do that because you were a big boy and boys don't cry, and anyway, it was only a movie and besides that, you *are* the breeze!

Sometimes at night, when the wind was quite right and my blood was a mixture of weed and the speed of adrenaline from doing endless martial arts cadas, I felt my being extending. It was like I could just send out my feelers all around, and move on the wind. I would just know—by a perturbation in the chi field—if Ripoff was coming around. I had enlisted the insects — they were each a lens of his many-faceted compound eyes — out there in the dark, peeping, sensing, keeping an eye on all that part of the meadow for me. My consciousness had moved back into a poly-sensate awareness. I had become the Knight of a Thousand Eyes.

Mother Nature had accepted me. I was one of her helpers. I had become a servant. I was a servant of the weed, and in turn weed would become my servant. It was the oldest, simplest, most direct relationship there was. I had found my part in the scheme of things.

There is nothing more beautiful than doing Tai Chi while high out on a big meadow under the sky—to be shadowboxing the space around your Self, irrigating the joints, while balanced and precariously spinning on one heel, leaping into flying kicks.

I have pulled together some thoughts on doing tai chi; unfortunately the beginning student needs to wax philosophical. Chi is such

a big change of paradigm and I of course had to take this to unbelievable lengths. I had a few books I had picked up in San Francisco and
Berkeley. I had a lot of time on my hands that summer and I started
figuring out how to make some Chinese ideograms using the typewriter thinking that there was something about the way the ideograms for the tai chi moves are built out of basic set of strokes that
would also lend insight. I just kept trying to get it down into a kind
of more and more basic set of elements. I needed to build myself a
kind of mnemonic theatre, in order to remember the moves and I
wanted it to be a kind of generative mnemonic theatre, because I
didn't have any craven images to place on the wall of my mnemonic
theatre. So the generative elements became hexagrams as you will
see.*

I also got into Laban Notation. I got into these kind of space/
time/weight diagrams. I even made these little tai chi figures out of
characters on the typewriter to help me focus on the Form.

I also evolved a weird kind of grammar, that the line was like the
foot advancing and moving around. in which levels of movement
were bracketed and broken out.

When shadow boxing, one slowly explored forces and balance.
Scientifically, Tai Chi is an essay in resilience, in letting go of
rigidity, in seeing the lines of force and using them. It seeks to adapt,
not to interfere; to allow those lines of action to continue, not impact
with you. To find Grace, the sense of balance of the body. Grace! She
is so often tucked away and not called for, not given the opportunity
to exercise herself. Shadowboxing is an attempt to prolong and stay
in the state of grace.

* I have pulled the poems, narrative and essays together into a 3rd
volume titled: "Knight of a Thousand Eyes" --WU

138

Tai Chi attempts to draw chi, a kind of energy like that in the body electric, and other parts of the body, from the universe. The arms and legs fly out from the center and attempt, like a flower, to draw in and push out through this vital power, the internal energy of the body electric, or some other occult energy—the force of creativity itself perhaps—coursing through the universe.

The Tai chi player attracts this energy. By channeling this energy properly, by touching this pure, flowing energy of the watercourse way, and channeling a little of it in the service of nature. It the universe is a green dragon, then the tai chi player can for a moment find himself riding on this dragons back, at one with the force that through the green fuse drives Father Time—Mother Nature. Mom Nature, the female principle of the universe, and when you are doing Tai Chi you are dancing with her. She has an intoxicating hold on you, and you love her and she is strong enough to put you to sleep with just a touch in the right spot, and you are probing and probing for that right spot, with your weightlessness—to be, just for a minute, in Her, to become weightless, widthless, massless, to focus all your energy into a beam, and move it with pinpoint accuracy. (And incidentally, like the Vulcan, hopefully reach over and just turn this energy off in an adversary—hopefully.)

Sometimes He'd Dance at Night

Sometimes at night I would dance among the marijuana plants, wading into them, doing Tai Chi with them, with their energy, with the wind, pushing them, pulling on their long stems, stretching them out, closing my hand over their long buds and pulling off that sticky resin later to roll up into hash balls. The resin tasted spicy and hot like cinnamon or pepper. Time and I was wading into them, for they liked to be messed with and moved around, like girls on a dance floor. All the males had been offed, and there were only these husky females generating all this THC love juice. Leaning out for pollen that ...yearning for pollen that was never to come. Little Thais with their delicate turned up leaves. Tall Colombian beauties, bronzed Hawaiians.

Sometimes at night, when the wind was right, and it had whipped up the girls—I called them my girls, the roses of summer—I could almost hear them calling me, as if they were saying (very faintly filtered through wind, drifting on air).

"Come on City-boy."

"Come on Mr. City-boy."

"Come back and be with us."

To amuse myself I, the lonely shepherd keeping watch on his flock, the good shepherd leaning on his bo stick looking out into the starry night, wondered "What kind of a song would the marijuanas be singing out there in the field." The marijuana plants certainly would be much more closely in touch with Mother Nature. It would be Mothers Nature's song or some variation thereof.

It seemed to me the plants would have a very subdued range in their singing. It would be something like Gregorian chant. It would be a kind of work song of the females producing the THC, against this shifting chattering hiss of the summer cicadas sound. They were saying:

"Look."

"See."

"Here he comes."

"Sometimes he dances at night."

"He is coming, the fuzzy headed gardener."

"He is coming to pull the sticky resin from our colas."

The lovely THC the lovely THC

We are making the sticky resiny THC

pull us off, we are loaded with THC

wet buds, wet colas

sticky fingers holding up the THC

the fertile fertile Marijuana

religious golden THC

The plants had only one note. I began to think of or imagine I could hear the females singing this work song, this kind of Gregorian chant of the marijuana patch to each other, against the jungle aliveness of the night.

the yearning tumbles out,

and rises high in the thrall currents

the yearning: "O we are so full of resin,

hurry we are so full of resin. Fertilize us!"

"We are the sexy intellectual sativa females

wet with golden religious THC".

praise be the THC

rolled up in the joints

praise be the THC in the joints

Marijuanas are gorgeous prostitutes

sold by their pimps for pleasure

we want to be more desirable

we want to be more sexy

we want to be more Mary, d'ya wanna?

taste the marijuana

take the marijuana in

taste the marijuana

"Here is the sexy resin."

"Here is the sticky psychoactivity."

The price of marijuana is rising

is rising

is rising

$75 for an 1/8th

that's $600 an ounce

OUCH!

that's inflation

already more precious than gold

soon joints will roll out of old cigarette machines

for 3 times the cost of a carton!

•••

The hoards of locusts had gone by now, and the patch was so dense that when I walked among the plants I would bump into them and sashay into them and their resins would rub off on me. These were the most beautiful females you could ever imagine.

One day I shouted with joy: "These are sativa! the sexy intellectual stone!"

"Yer damn right!" Gregory shouted back in agreement. "Not that killer rub-your-dick-in-the-dirt sleepy skunk weed indica that they grow out in California. I hate that stuff."

"It puts me to sleep." I said.

"Me, too."

"You know why they grow that stuff, don't you?" Greg said.

"No, no I don't. Why."

"The growers in California are connoisseurs of oblivion. This kind of pot was developed by the downer generation who raised Quaalude obviousness to a lifestyle."

"You think that's it? I argued. "There's supposed to be some spiritual people in California."

"OK, well maybe." Greg allowed. "In all fairness I have to say that this kind of weed was not just an invention of people with downer syndrome. There was greed. They hybridized indica from the hash bush out of shear economic greed. It grows faster so you don't need to be exposed to the danger as much. Or you can grow several crops in one year. Because it is smaller, it doesn't take so long to flower, it looks potent as hell, and it has that ripe skunk weed odor that, for people who don't know any better, means it is more potent."

"Bummer."

"Yea, right, bummer."

19

THE SONG OF MARYJANE

On the land I'd spend a lot of time in fantasy. I'd spend hours working the writer's magic of keeping my spirits high and keeping the momentum going continuing to work on my book *Sex is the Anti-Gravity of Metamorphosis.* I'd imagine that it was finished, and that it was a success. I'd imagine that they had sent out this smart sympathetic literate young woman journalist to conduct a field interview of me.

It was a pretty elaborate fantasy. She'd be walking around in the fields, wearing khaki fatigues with a portable tape recorder slung over her shoulder.

She's a lovely young woman, probably 28, a few years knocking around working her way up doing a little voice-over work, commercials, and short pieces until she became a radio journalist. She likes my writing; I am flirting with her. She is not only beautiful but one of my biggest fans. She has these romantic inclinations toward me. I first met this woman when I was being taken out to lunch at a literary cafe by my publisher. This woman Veronica Verdun was in the group. At the cabaret Woody Allen was sitting-in with his clarinet. We ordered glasses of claret and through its amber lens our eyes met in shining admiration and recognition and understanding, and Veronica Verdun lifted her glass toward me and the others followed and she said, "Here's to Walker Underwood. We are so glad to have you writing for us in America."

And I felt all this confirmation and acceptance, not to mention money.

"I am here visiting Walker Underwood the nature poet at his farm outside Manor, Texas," she'd say into the mike.

"He has just published a volume of narrative poems, or is it a lyrical novel, *Sex is the Anti-Gravity of Metamorphosis*.

"Well, basically it's a story about the creative process," I would say.

"I'm looking out at the lush verdant plants of Walker's pot patch," she would say. "This is beautiful. It is about half the size of a football field! The plants are beautiful, big and bushy."

"They are hefty, aren't they?" I would add.

"You've got a lot of marijuana growing out here," she'd say.

"Yea, I've got all kinds, too. Those tall darker ones there, are Hawaiians. And those over there with the delicate leaves are Thais."

"Those big hefty ones are Colombians. "

"And they are sinsimilla?" she'd ask.

"Of course. They're all females. These are my girls. I've started referring to them as my girls."

I'd bring Veronica up close to the plants for a look. I'd pull a large cola down for her to inspect the flowers up close. The marijuana flowers oozed thick droplets of amber liquor that glistened in the moon-light, breaking light up into its colors, giving them almost a sheeny aura. The buds were frothy with THC oil that matted their hairs back. This gave them a bad-to-the-bone look.

"Look at how well they are producing," I'd say.

The interviewer lady, who was not only good looking but literate, surprised me by quoting from my poetry.

"You have a scene in your poem *The Song of Maryjane*: "He waded through the marijuana patch whose plants were taller than a man. His spirit rose and exalted as he breathed in the THC-drenched air.""

"Yesss..., how kind of you to remember," I'd demur.

"So this is the patch where you wrote that you could hear the song of Maryjane."

"Yes"

"How did that come about?"

"Well I had to kind of develop my own hybrid aesthetic of poetry."

"Yes and what is that," she'd pursue.

"I call it poetry as communion."

"Poetry as communion....poetry as communion. What does that mean."

"Well, basically it can be summed up in the dictum, 'A writer is a machine for turning drugs into poems.'" I would smile sheepishly in mock earnestness.

"You've probably experienced it," I continued, "if you've ever done acid or other hallucinogenic drugs. It's kind of a hippie aesthetic. You feel like you can become things. It's like getting closer and closer to the phenomena. To somehow resonate with it. They could do that in the old poetry. I wanted to be like the writers of the old poetry. These writers could become things. Even as late as Ezra Pound, you have, "Me thought I was a tree amid the woods / and many things became clear to me / that were rank folly to my head before".

"I guess I'd have to sum it up by saying, in order to study nature on its own terms, that is, as they say in the old poetry, to "become" a cloud, or to "be" a tree or some other work of nature, it is necessary to do drugs. To partake in nature this way is to... to transcend your own physical being and through the imagination, resonate with the silent imagination at work in the heart of all nature."

"Ooooh, I love it when you talk like that," she'd say, a little embarrassed about talking about drugs openly on the radio. She'd give me a knowing hippie smile.

And then becoming emboldened by my disclosure she'd say, "Yeah, I can relate to that."

"I remember doing acid with my boyfriend once, and we were so high and together and in love and so vulnerable and sensitive to it all and we went down to the pond to look at the swans and thought we were able to see through the eyes of the swans."

"Yes, exactly."

"Well, what did you find here in the patch." she'd say further pursuing the interview.

"Here, let me show you."

I pulled a country joint—rolled tight at both ends—out of my jean shirt.

"Now in order to hear the *Song of Maryjane* you have to be in a proper state. Here, we'll field test some of my home grown."

She was one of those women who enjoyed a smoke and her eyes would light up at the thought of getting turned on, but she enjoyed teasing me and having me on, "You have to approach it with an open mind." she said with a wink.

"That's right," I would say, playing along. We'd grin knowingly at each other. "And this is something that will open your mind."

Sitting side by side on the cot under the tree I torched it up with a flick of my bic.

"Is this some of your own home grown?" she'd say.

"Yep."

After we had done smoking it, I'd nonchalantly lean over and say to her, real low, so that she might not get it and it would go over her head and he wouldn't have to deal with it, "They sing to me when I dance with them.

"Who."

"The plants."

She'd look at me incredulously

"You just sit there and I'll wade into them," I'd say, "and you see if you can get it on tape."

As I started to wade into the pot patch which was so thick I had to move one plant aside to slip by to get to the next, the harmonium of my girls' voices would slowly drift in from inaudibility and well up from among themselves and drift about on wisps of air.

"My God! I've got to catch this on tape," she'd exclaim, pointing her microphone toward the patch. The sound wafted over, ever so faintly, and sweetly—filtered through wind, drifting on air: a chorus of girls' voices.

As this phenomenon was occurring, she started giving a real time description of it into her tape —in her best radio voice: "As we sat out in the windy pot patch, we heard their music which seemed to well up from among the plants. It was the voices of the marijuana plants in his pot patch, singing to him as he walked through them."

The lovely THC the lovely THC
We are making the sticky resiny THC
pull us off, we are loaded with THC
wet buds, wet colas
sticky fingers holding up the THC
the fertile fertile Marijuana
religious golden THC

"The plants have only one note," she'd complain.

"Yes It's a kind of Gregorian chant of the marijuana patch." I would say. "What did you expect, Reggae? These are hard working, serious, spiritual beings. This is their work song. It's an old chain gang Gregorian chant blues."

She'd be shocked, trying to disbelieve her ears. Not only was she having an audio hallucination of singing plant, but some guy is here telling her about what kinds of songs they sing.

"Apparently," she'd say trying to rationalize the phenomenon, "these are state specific aural acoustic phenomena, requiring that the observer be in the right state."

Her eyes were wide, her mouth going round, in a gasp of amazement, but she is a professional journalist, she is getting it all down on tape: a choir of girls' voices sweetly filtered through wind, drifting on air.

The sexy intellectual is melted,
all that color all that space
partake in us
as we partake in you
breath the space in; breath the space out
taste, feel
"Here is the sexy resin."
"The mind's untied released
sets sail in a sea of paradigms adrift,
and reels in an ocean of sunshine."

She was dumfounded and visibly shaken. Her voice spoke in a quavering far off way. She was stunned and shocked. "Wow, how have you been able to handle this," she'd say, sympathetically, having experienced a little of it herself now.

"Well Veronica, I have prepared myself for this. I've studied all the kinds of poetry: narrative, lyric, meditative, ancient and modern. Even the latest incantatory expansionist poems. The Song of Maryjane is one by the way. I've studied objectivist poems, "Deep Image" poems, "Deep Ecology" poems, concrete and minimal works, I've studied them all."

"I was just so hungry to create that I had to get myself into a state where I could just go out into nature and take dictation. I think art should be more phenomenological and less humanistic. I don't mean to be offensive but we have too long been manipulated by stars and media. Commercial media over-stimulates, it is good for the stars and the owners of media but it is not good for us. We can't find ourselves in it. What I wanted to do is try to find my place in the universe, to feel the universe with its natural rhythms in my life. I think we might find out that phenomenological art is the most humanistic of all. I wanted to get closer to the phenomena. To somehow resonate with it. Like they did in the old poetry."

"It isn't easy to for us to observe the underlying reality of things — to know that marijuana is, for example, oversexed."

"And it isn't easy knowing that crickets and grasshoppers are able to make easy transmissions to other planets."

I thought for a moment about the preposterousness of that statement and thought better of it and qualified it with, "That is what they are trying to do, anyway—trying to harmonize and get into sympathetic vibration with the background white noise of the universe and send messages to other planets."

"How do you know this?" She'd ask suspiciously.

"I don't know if any one of them have ever done it, but they have informed me of how they are trying."

"It takes a lot of patience for them to get a whole sentence out because they are always clambering all over each other at once and they have a horrendous stuttering problem."

20

CATERWAULING AT THE SPEED OF LIGHT

Then in my fantasy Veronica and I are back in her studio at the radio station, doing some more interview. Her show has some weird name like "Be My Consideration".

The theme song for "Be My Consideration" comes up. It is a bright forceful musical bed. As it fades down, Veronica says, "Welcome to Be My Consideration."

Even in my own fantasy there is a weird coloration I couldn't explain: Although Veronica was from southern California, she affected a BBC accent for her radio talk show. But I was going along with it, because I wanted to start my own radio program. The Radio Dude Ranch of the Air.

"From Veronica Verdun it's Hello and welcome along to today's edition of the program."

"At the microphone today I have Walker Underwood who comes from Austin, Texas." She says "Austin, Texas" disdainfully. She catches herself up and becomes brusque and businesslike. "Walker is a writer and poet who lives in the country.

"Welcome aboard, Walker."

And I, a bit slower, suspicious, southern say, "OK. Uh, thanks. This is great to be here, Veronica."

And then I say, flirting, hustling, hopeful, "Do you call yourself Veronica or Ronnie."

"Veronica will be fine," she says, emphatic and deadpan, cutting me off.

Then quickly, smoothly, professionally she takes control and says, "Walker, how did you first find that writing and poetry was the thing you wanted to do."

I got this image of himself sitting at an old dark brown wooden desk in Catholic school. "I think it was when I was in the 3rd grade," I say. "I remember we had lists of words that we had to use in sentences.

"I just loved putting words into sentences. I would make these great long sentences whose meaning twisted and turned through two and three and then all the words in the list. Then I'd have to wrap my mind around the reality. I love where it took me.

"I don't know. For me it just created another kind of reality. (Some place other than where I was)."

Veronica looks at me. Her eyes are shining with recognition at the struggle of the child.

I continued: "Up until that time I had actually wanted to be an artist. I can recall my first understanding of that. It happened in the apartment I lived in with my parents. It was in a nice 50s modern room and there was sunlight coming through high windows. I must have been about 3 or 4, and of course the windows were high. I was looking at a painting on the wall. We had a painting of a sail boat on an ocean in our apartment. It was one of those romantic lyrical paintings where the artist had laid the paint on thick in the ocean part like it was waves.

"Now I had this favorite uncle I loved very much and trusted. He sat me down in front of the painting of the boat on the ocean one day and said, 'If you look at that picture long enough the boat and the water will seem to move.'

152

"And I decided to try it out one day. I spent a long time in the apartment by myself looking at the picture, and sure enough and to my great shock it *did* begin to move. It was one of those impressionistic paintings with a great heaving sea, and I was a little frightened and thrown off balance by this. I remember thinking 'I'm not supposed to see this!' In fact it was kind of horrible because now every time I looked over at the painting on the wall in our apartment for longer than a glance it would start to move. Almost like it was mocking me, or teasing me, or challenging me. It began to take on a kind of life of its own in my young mind."

Turning back to Veronica, I say, "So after seeing that and realizing what a power it was for a person to be able to create these magical windows that hung on the wall and can capture light and motion, I wanted to be an artist.

"It wasn't until I was in the third grade writing class that I realized that a writer could also be an artist too, and it was then that I wanted to become a writer."

Veronica says "My, what a gift that uncle gave you,"

Realizing it for the first time, I say, "Yes, it was a gift."

Veronica, feeling the pressure to move the show along says, "What happened next? How did your writing develop from that?"

"It wasn't until high school and adolescent angst that poetry really started meaning something to me." I say.

"That was back in the days of the beatniks. I... one day I threw all my books into a locker in San Antonio and hitchhiked up to New York city to see some beatniks. I had had enough of school and was going to **experience** what it meant to really *exist*."

"Oh, break a mother's heart." Veronica says, in a chiding, teasing way.

I felt chagrined at the thought of my mother's heart breaking, (once again!) "Yes, it was pretty drastic," I said.

Veronica turns away to speak directly to the folks in radioland. "Walker has been experimenting with natural poetry and sounds. He's also recorded them on tape.

"You've brought some of your recordings to the studio today?"

"Uh, yes I have, Veronica. I have some recordings of the cicada and frog symphony."

Veronica, rocked back and forth in her seat, and clapped her hands with joy. "O swell. What's first?"

"Well, I've put together a piece that traces the movement of an afternoon. But since we don't have an afternoon to listen to the whole symphony I've pulled together some of the ideas in it here."

Veronica, sensing my nervousness moved to facilitate, "Tell us a little about the selection you are going to play."

"It tries to give the sense of slow time. But I need to draw you in. To show you how to see the patterns in the soundscape. So I'll lead you into the symphony by pointing out traditional elements in it, like duets and trios and ensemble and polyphony, and then I'll play a raga for you to show about moving in a tone row of harmonies and we'll also look at an idea in gamalon music.

"My, that sounds like quite an eclectic musical journey," Veronica say. "What do you call it."

"Oh, it's got a great long and ponderous title," I say. Then, taking a deep breath, drawing myself up erect and pausing for effect say it slowly as if it were wafting on the breath, "Like a Mirage moving across a Landscape in Spring Time."

I pause and look at her face, waiting for it to sink in.

Veronica rests her chin on the palm of her hand in a thoughtful

154

pose. "Like a Mirage? Moving across a Landscape in Spring Time. She said each word distinctly, one word at a time. Then putting it all together, she says a little more slowly musing, getting it: "Like a Mirage moving across a Landscape in Spring Time!

"How intriguing. Tell us a little about..." and this time she says it with an emphatic flourish of her hand, as if it were a banner waving in air, "Like a Mirage moving across a Landscape in Spring Time."

I think: It is time to let the work speak for itself. "OK," I say, "I'm going to start playing a bit of it and then focus in on a few aspects of it to help you hear it."

The Mirage Symphony

The basic forest mix fades up. The Mirage Symphony—a background of sound from cicadas and crickets going at it loud on a hot summer's night.

"This first part is a leitmotif," I say, "it introduces the instruments. You will see it start with the crickets, then lead into the cicadas, and frogs."

A wall of variegated white noise sounds wafts over them in wave like patterns of increasing and decreasing density, droning.

"I have used an automated mix to pan along the edges of the droning, focusing the background down, and bringing up individual sounds out of the mix. This kind of crossfade-pan combination has the effect of zooming or focusing a particular sound out of the background sound localizing it naturally in 3D space. Like an ear was an eye focusing or localizing a sound. You might think of it in terms of graphic design: text mapped to a curve."

We listen to this for a while.

After a few moments I ask, "Can you find the highest sound in

155

the piece? Here I'll focus it in for you. They are like the piccolos."

The basic forest mix fades down, and the high cricket and cicadas mix fades up.

"I have also mixed in what I call the sound beam: a hard edged cicada trill slightly retarded between left and right so that it is like a beam of sound passing across the space between the ears. It is like a flashlight of sound, searching and probing."

This plays for a while, then it crossfades back to the basic forest mix.

"Can you find the base?" I suggest. "Here I'll focus it in for you."

At this point on the tape, the basic forest mix fades down, and the low part of frogs comes up then fades back into the mix.

"Then there is the midrange," I say, "the chorus of the frog symphony." The frog symphony around a pond starts really going.

As the sound fades back to the basic forest mix, Veronica interrupts, "So. These are the instruments of your symphony."

"Yes, Veronica"

At this point on the tape, the a-lap part of a raga begins slowly mixing with the white noise of the cicadas and cricket basic mix. The droning strings of the tamboura come to the fore. The raga—with its movement through subtle timbrel color changes, and its sympathetic strings reacting to the primary strings—reflects the similar kind of movement in the basic forest mix.

"I have put a little raga music alongside the mix," I say, "because I want the listener to start looking for patterns moving through the sound. What you will see are these streams of harmonics running through the sound. You get a sense of movement—a subtle movement, a shifting, a shimmering—of the tone colors."

156

Veronica says, "Oh, how interesting."

"Yes, it is quite a different aesthetic." I agree. "These ragas are played at different times of the day, and they have different harmonic colorations depending on the time of the day. This is something our ancient insect musicians taught the ancient human musicians."

At this point on the tape the Raga drone fades down and the Forest Mix fades back up.

"I'd like to show you one more different aesthetic," I say, "that the insect musicians taught the human musicians."

"What's that." Veronica asks

We start hear the sound of gamalon Kay-Chack slowly emerge in a cross fade from the basic forest mix. Once can definitely recognize these are humans chanting/shouting.

As the kay-chack is slowly coming up out of the mix, I say, "Well, you know the frogs and insects don't take extended solos. Their music is tribal, more like group chanting."

Veronica and I listen for a while. I slide a picture of a group of Balinese chanting men out of a folder and show it to her. "These people get all huddled up around each other," I tell her, "like they are riding a luge, all together. They sway back and forth with each other chanting. It must be really high."

"Oh my," she say, "they do look like they are quite hunkered down around it, don't they."

The basic forest mix fades down to silence. I say, "OK, so the next thing we've got to do is try to visualize the overall physical process from the sound." At this point on the tape, the sound of the wind rifling and filtering through trees softly plays, "Like for example, in this part here.

"Here is where the wind slowly comes up and it reaches out like with a million fingers and plays the leaves as if they were keys on an instrument."

Veronica and I listen quietly to this beautiful sound. A smile spreads across Veronica's face, as she is getting the image with the sound.

I continue conducting, "Now here is the part where we can follow the wind as it blows over the land, in other words the whole field becomes the resonance cavity of the wind's instrument. The wind is like the primary strings and the insects and the leaves are the secondary strings.

"But it takes a long time for that sense of it to creep up on you."

At this point the leitmotif on the tape fades down to silence.

"That was the leitmotif," I say. "The whole symphony takes hours. I have just given you a speeded-up taste of it."

But if I was to try and sum up the sense of it in an image I'd say it is a feeling of the creatures in a meadow soundscape trying to catch Summer as it moves swiftly by.

"But of course you have to listen to this over a long period time. It's something you have to acquire a taste for, like raga music."

Veronica and I listened to the synopsis symphony with me occasionally pointing out, musical aspects, "Now, here I want you to notice the polyphony."

Where there is a call and response going, I point out various duets; of two crickets, trios; with "I think it might be a trio of a cicada and two crickets," then a trio of frogs.

I tell her about resonating with the heat, and about how people who live in the country and live with this cicada sound all the time, get their nervous system slowed down and they get locked into the

158

rhythm of the work.

"What work is that?" Veronica asks

"Their own work," I say, "and the work of the universe."

"I see." Veronica say.

Then feeling like she has to move the show along, Veronica says, "I understand you have actually been able to conduct some of these insect musicians in the field."

I am a little shocked at her bringing this up, "Well, Veronica, it's not so much that I am able to go out into the field and conduct them, but, it turns out they do respond to radio (as well as lawn mowers, chains saws and jackhammers).

"I mean, I did once put a radio controlled recorder out in the field, and then fired up a chain saw back at the house to see what effect it would have, and it definitely did have an effect. But what I am doing here is more that I am kind of a musical guide and I will be like a docent and talk you through the musical aspects of their art as it is happening."

Turning back to the audience in radio land, Veronica says, "Well..." and then looking at the clock exclaims, "Oh we're just about out of time," and then after a pause says, "That about raps it up for today. That's all the time we have."

The radio theme gradually comes up as Veronica says, "Be sure to stay tuned for my next guest on Be My Consideration."

Veronica turns to me and says, "Thank you very much Walker."

My reply: "I really appreciate that these cicadas get a chance to be on the air. Cause then they really do get to propagate their cater-wauling at the speed of light to other planets."

The radio theme gradually comes all the way up and we fade out.

21

LIKE A COYOTE OUT ON THE PRAIRIE IN A HAILSTORM

The spell of the Maryjane Rose is a spell so high and wild it will scramble space and time if you let it.

Gregory and I had already started the harvest and had half a dozen precociously potent plants hanging upside down, drying in the old tackle shed. We were sitting under the tree on the back patio drinking lemonade when I heard the helicopter hovering whove whove whove whove whove like some giant mix master, its blades chopping space and time—hovering over and over out back by the pot patch— there, treading air dreadfully, drubbing doom.

It was like some giant horrendous mechanical insect looking huge and horrible some 50 feet in the air over the pot patch— a helicopter. For an instant I wondered if Big G had come alive. The helicopter was angled down, looking, scrutinizing the pot patch through its huge bubble insect eyes.

Suddenly we knew.

"Oh no! It's a bust!!"

I didn't know what to do. We knew we didn't really have a chance to run for it. We'd have to go through thick brush; the laws would have the dogs and helicopters chasing us. There was a good chance we would get shot. All my stuff was here and the place was in my name. The authorities could lock it up and stake it out forever. My heart sunk as the realization set in. The situation was like that old coyote out on the prairie in the middle of a hailstorm, no place to run, no place to hide—this was one of those situations where you just had to lie down, put your paws over your ears and take it. We would just have to get busted.

The police would be coming up the long driveway soon, so we had only a few minutes. Turned out they cut the lock with bolt cutters. We put Butch and the dobies inside so they wouldn't get shot. Greg and I took down the half dozen plants we had drying and the little bit that was already manicured, snapped it into shorter lengths and stuffed it into a plastic bag. We knew the police would look all through the house. Gregory took the little stash out to his safe cache—a garbage pail buried under ground, with a board and dirt on top of that, and a stone on top of that.

Then I started worrying about, "What should we do to get prepared for jail."

"I don't know, I've never been there," said Greg.

"Me, neither."

"Well," I said, "mom always said to wear clean underwear." We started putting on clean underwear and socks.

"I've heard it's really cold in there with the air conditioning," Gregory said.

So I put on a couple of undershirts too. I stuck my toothbrush in my back pocket.

Soon some of Austin's finest were swarming. A DPS deputy, was out of the shoot first with pump shotgun in hand, running along beside their still moving car, yelling, "Hands up!" He leveled the roomsweeper at Greg and I. Two more officers jumped out of their cars. They quickly crouched behind open car doors and pointed enormous .38 service revolvers at us. Out of car three, came two more braves. Very big beefy fellows, wearing stiffly starched uniforms over bullet-proof vests, they were easily closer to 300 pounds than 200.

What the peace warriors encountered was two nice, long-haired, young, gentleman farmers sitting up straight in old metal lawn chairs on the front porch, their hands in plain view resting on the porch rail. Greg and I tried to look innocent. Our dogs were barking inside.

"Turn around and face the wall! Put your hands on the wall! You're under arrest!"

The dogs went wild. Butch the extremely kind and gentle little border collie had his teeth bared. The two Dobermans, Hijo and Ada were climbing the walls in the bedroom. Some cops came up on the front porch. From then on, it was all standard procedure. "Hands up against the wall, feet spread!" The splatter gun moved in closer as they frisked Gregory and I. A steady stream of peace officers pulled their cars up to the gathering. Greg and I stood with our hands against the wall in the heat of this, the most awful of August dog days, until our feet got tired.

"IT SURE WOULD BE NICE IF WE COULD SIT DOWN!" bellowed Greg.

"You better keep your hands up there and your mouth shut," said the cop.

Then the main man, who's bust this was, pulled up. As he got out of his car, and walked toward the house, he saw that I had my hat on, and so he went back into the squad car and got his white Stetson. Then, proffering his badge and card toward me he said, "Oh, by the way, I don't know if you've seen one of these." I read the name. Renee Martin, he was part Mexican. Greg and I, in our handcuffs, were seated on the front porch. The cuffs made us lean forward in a very subservient position.

162

"Who lives here," a big mean looking fellow with beard and long hair and scraggly looking van Dyke beard said.

"I do," I said.

They kept coming up the steps. Sheriffs, policemen, constables, deputies and one exceedingly obsequious little chicken shit police follower who said he was a freelance reporter with the Houston Chronicle. I took a particular dislike to him.

The sun beat down and Greg and I writhed uncomfortably in our seats.

It was like an aweful rape. I remembered the advice Malcolm X gave for these situations: you what to try and appear as an equal man. Try to relate to them on a human level and they will try to relate to you. "There's a big jug of cold water in the fridge," I said. I was trying to relate to them on a human level. I had heard that for women in the rape situation the best thing for her to do is to act inhuman: to get down on her hands and knees and start eating handfuls of grass, or to pick her nose or otherwise do something to totally turn the guy off. Whereas a man should try to relate on a more human level, try to find areas of common expertise. Unfortunately the only thing I could think of that we had in common was lawbreaking and marijuana cultivation.

A cop recited to us, reading from a little laminated card, the beautiful poem of Miranda.

One cop named Mike was really fucked-up. He came up onto the porch with the machete. He sat there with it hacking dully on the wood railing looking menacing, while his coworkers searched the grounds.

The laws walked us back to the patch. The cops wrestled with the pot plants jerking them back and forth until they wrenched some of them out of the ground. That was too much work so they brought out chain saws and hacked up the beautiful females while Greg and I stood there with our hands handcuffed behind our backs having to watch the massacre. Four big men worked for a couple of hours with machetes hacking. I thought I could hear my unborn babies cry. Gregory turned around and looked the other way in disgust.

"Why's he crying," asked the reporter, nodding toward Gregory.

I looked and sure enough Gregory, all 6'2", 175 pounds of him was walking around, shaking his head and crying openly. It was quite a sight. Youth will be crushed. They filled up the whole back of a pick-up truck with pot plants. It was mounded up over the top of the cab and weighing it down.

They took Greg and me into town and the process began.

I remember talking to the cop in the car as we drove in. It felt good to get into the air conditioning. I said, "Someday they will think back on this as prohibition and see how wrong it was filling our jails with people trying to explore consciousness."

He said, "Yea, you might be right. Could be you're ahead of your time." He kind of chuckled at the pun.

I wanted to shout at him and the ranchers and others as we drove past and who I imagined knew we were disgraced. I wanted to tell them somethig about the wildness of this place. I felt like saying

Hey!

Hey you there!

Yes, I see you over there in your big cylindrical silos of gleaming aluminum full of cattlefeed.

You've got white rail fences all around

You've got your crops and garden planted straight, row upon row.

You don't even know I exist.

I smoke marijuana and I'm invisible to you.

No I need to tell them what they are looking at.

You look at a puddle or you look at the folds in the land or you look at the tree as it is reaching up it's twig tips and you think you know what it is but you don't.

You think they are just matter here to serve you, but you're wrong, they're beings, entities all moving apace. Full of feelings and designs and yes of love.

Man you just don't see it and you never will.

I put myself on automatic pilot. It was all just too disgusting. At the highway patrol office I remembered a lyric from a Bob Dylan song: *Walking upside down inside hand-cuffs / What else can you show me.* I needed to make a gesture of defiance, no matter what the consequences. I bent over as if to pick something up, placed the palms of my hands squarely on the cold marble precinct floor, and even though my hands were held precariously close together by the handcuffs, I managed to do a handstand. I then amazed the assembled police, clerks, secretaries, and anyone else who saw it, to see this tall long-haired man, dangling upside down, hefting his weight up from one hand to the other, moving slowly in halting, staggering, quivering, balancing moves across the hallway as I did indeed walk upside down on my hands while in handcuffs.

We got booked. We got our mug shots taken with a number written on a slate that hung from the neck on a chain. We were put into jail. I was by himself in an ugly cell in downtown Austin.

The bunk was a solid slab of steel. They put an old drunk cowboy in there with me. The old cowboy went to lie down on the bunk and immediately jumped up and dusted off his duff saying, "I do believe that is the hardest bunk I have ever sat on."

They gave you a blanket. When I looked out through the bars I saw cages going of into the distance as far as the eye could see, tier upon tier spreading infinitely in all directions, like some great tessellation extruded by society. I whiled away a little time scratching mathematical equations in the thick, hideous, peach-colored, multilayered paint covering the metal cell wall. I thought of the Jewish mathematician Banach occupying his mind and escaping his pain by inventing discontinuous topological spaces while in a concentration camp during the 2nd World War. It was like being in a submarine or something all this metal and pipes.

Lenora got us a smart Jewish lawyer and we were let out the next day.

I felt totally raped. I had no place to stay and only 7 cents in my pocket when I got out of jail. I walked along Waller creek where it runs through the campus. I had graduated 13th in my class, in physics only a few years earlier. I felt mighty low; all that promise gone to waste. I knew Butch would not make it in the city. I did not want to go back out to the farm ever again but I had to go back several times to settle Butch with the new renters.

In court for the preliminary hearing, I was surprised to recognize the judge as somebody I had known in college. I remembered him as a big burly hippie guy, always wearing a raggedy T-shirt and with a big Rasputin beard. As a college student this man had been an organizer for the SDS—Students for a Democratic Society— which back in the those days was a communist youth organization, and here it turned out that he had gone all through law school and become a judge. Now he looked magnificent, had the trim beard of the Schweppes bitter lemon man, and looked steely eyed, in a double breasted blue serge suite under his black robes, presiding over my case.

The prosecution brought forth the photos—glossy, $8^1/_2$ x 11 color photos suitable for framing—taken from the air. I craned my neck to get a look. God, it was so obvious; we had been so stupid. There in a vast sea of dry, burnt out weeds stood a lovely oasis of moist green, and, O Jesus, there was the giant grasshopper standing by the house! Where did I think I was! The prosecution said they had taken over 200 plants of good sinsimilla worth an estimated $400,000.

The judge looked at the prosecution and shook his head. He picked up one of the pictures and rapped it sharply with the back of his finger nails and said: "You had to fly beneath 500 feet in order to recognize this is marijuana.

"Without proper warrant, you violated this man's air space."

The judge glanced at the prosecutor with a kind of sympathetic disdain, making his point in a weary tone as if he had tried to teach this lesson before.

"A person ought to be able to expect a reasonable amount of privacy in their own garden. I discharge this case for incorrectly obtained evidence."

I could have thrown myself down on his knees and kissed the judge's hand in gratitude. Ah, once again I was free.

HiT MoteL Press

www.hitmotel.com
These books can be ordered from any book seller or on-line .
Check www.hitmotel.com for selections and recordings.

Boho Novels
The Little House on the Prairie Trilogy:
Cultivating the Texas Twister Hybrid, a portrait of the artist as a weed
gardener (1998) ISBN 0-9655842-0-8 $20.00
The Secret of the Cicadas' Song, a peyote trip in poetry and prose (1998)
ISBN 0-9655842-1-6 $20.00
Knight of 1000 eyes, about Tai Chi, movement, Laban, and the I Ching
(1998) ISBN 0-9655842-2-4 $20.00

The Punctual Actual Weekly, about the life and times of a small mimeo-
graph literary rag centered around artists living in a Berkeley warehouse
and the Amphictionic Theatre (2000) ISBN 0-9655842-8-3
The Church of the Coincidental Metaphor, youthful adventures in Mexican
radio ISBN 0-9655842-7-5
The Indigenous Tribesmen of Neverland, bohemian life in Austin slacker
enclaves (1999) ISBN 0-9655842-6-7 $20.00
Sex is the Anti-gravity of Metamorphosis, tales of romance and despair
hitchhiking in US, Canada and Mexico. (1999) ISBN 0-9655842-9-1

Novels:
My Years of Apprenticeship at Love Trilogy:
Dolores Park, Texan joins a California Tantric Buddhist commune (1999)
ISBN 0-9655842-3-2 $20.00
The Jung of University Avenue, a journal of psychotherapy
(1999) ISBN 0-9655842-4-0
A Blue Moon in August, about marriage and children late in life. (1999)
ISBN 0-9655842-5-9

CD-ROM
Cultivating the Texas Twister Hybrid CD-ROM, radio plays of actor's
voices performing bits from the novels, the Mirage Symphony

Nonfiction
The Diamond Cutter's Sutra, about semiotics, logic, semantic object
modeling, mathematics --a kind of Varieties of Logical Experience

Check into HiT MoteL chat and framed presentation about emergent
complexity constantly drifting through. @www.hitmotel.com

Check out this audio CD from **HiT MoteL** Press

Cultivating the Texas
Twister Hybrid

Set against the music of storms, winds, and the natural environment of cicadas, crickets, frogs and birds these radio plays enacted by voice-over actors speaking lines from novels by Michael Lyons present a very special 3D sound experience. In particular the Mirage Symphony shows how a symphonic structure imbues the ambient sounds of the world, indicating a dialog or a thought in the universal mind.

Catman in Dogwalk House
Loafers of the Kandinsky Sound Museum
The Background Hiss of Summer
Stockhausen
Somtimes He'd Dance at Night
Caterwalling at the Speed of Light
The Mirage Synphony
Oxygen
Green Bank Parade

You can read the script and listen to samples from the radio play on the website at

www.hitmotel.com

HiT MoteL Press

presents these other books in the series by Michael Lyons

Cultivating the Texas Twister Hybrid is the first book. It is about the adventures of a city guy on a farm growing weed. It is a gardener's journal teaching the growers craft and something of the connoisseurs's educations as well as a criminal's internal monolog.

Cultivating the Texas Twister Hybrid

Michael Lyons

The Secret of the Cicadas' Song

Michael Lyons

The Secret of the Cicadas' Song is another books about an event on the farm. It is an extended peyote trip in prose and poetry. The time of the book is a peyote trip. One is brought to the immediacy of the experience through haiku poetry and to the ineffable aspect of the experience through object verse and semantic object modeling of the archetypes of perception.

Knight of 1000 eyes is another books about an event on the farm. The time of the book is a tai chi session. It reflects the struggle of the western mind coming to understand the spirit of the universe. It has an essay on western space time motion philosopher Laban and a modern commentary on the ancient I Ching.

www.hitmotel.com

The Knight of 1000 eyes

Michael Lyons

to order directly from HiT MoteL by Mail go to the website and
1. Print this form.
2. mail this form with check or money order (made out to Michael Lyons) to:

HiT MoteL Press
2267 28th Ave.
San Francisco CA 94116

Name:_____

Address:_____

City:_____State:_____Zip:_____

Telephone:_____E-mail:_____

Title: Cultivating the Texas Twister Hybrid
ISBN 0-965542--0-8   @: $20 Qty:_____   Total:$_____

Title: The Secret of the Cicadas' Song
ISBN 0-965542--1-6   @: $20 Qty:_____   Total:$_____

Title: The Knight of 1000 eyes
ISBN 0-965542--2-4   @: $20 Qty:_____   Total:$_____

The Texas Twister CD-ROM
                       @: $20 Qty:_____   Total:$_____

                                      Sub Total:$_____

                       CA residents please add 8%:_____

                                      Shipping:_____

                                      Grand Total:_____

Shipping Information:
Shipping - Please add $3.50 for first item, $1.00 for each additional item
We ship via US Priority mail or UPS.

The Secret of the Cicadas' Song

The Secret of the Cicadas' Song is an extended internal monolog of a man walking through the fields on peyote.

Through semantics, semiotics, logic, fractals, chaos theory, sound, haiku, symbols, archetypes etc. the poem induces, a swooning nominal neumenal drug experience. We are present while the consciousness of the poem constructs various notation systems as the words in his language become objects.

One generative hypothesis of the poem is:

What would happen if Ezra Pound and Charles Dodson collaborated about being influenced by Wittgenstein, Hilbert, Dirac, Mandelbrot, Basho, Burroughs, Borges, Bukowski, Cendrars, Saunders...

The time of the book is a peyote trip. One is brought to the immediacy of the experience through haiku poetry and to the ineffable aspect of the experience through object verse and semantic object modeling of the archetypes of perception. The point of view shifts from the individual consciousness to the mind of Gaia.

$20.00 Literature / Philosophy / Poetry / Peyote
The HiT MoteL Press   **http://www.hitmotel.com**

www.ingramcontent.com/pod-product-compliance
Lightning Source LLC
Chambersburg PA
CBHW030329020726
47493CB00004B/1208